THE LORD OF THE SANDS OF TIME

ISSUI OGAWA

THE LORD OF THE SANDS OF TIME

ISSUI OGAWA

TRANSLATED BY JIM HUBBERT

HAIKA SORU

SAN FRANCISCO

HAIKASORU
Published by
VIZ Media, LLC
295 Bay Street
San Francisco, CA 94133

www.haikasoru.com

Ogawa, Issui, 1975-
  [Tokisuna no o. English]
  The lord of the sands of time/Issui Ogawa; translated by Jim Hubbert.
    p. cm.
  ISBN 978-1-4215-2762-8 (alk. paper)
  I. Hubbert, Jim. II. Title.
  PL874.G37J5713 2007
  895.6'35—dc22   2008051660

Printed in the U.S.A.
First printing, July 2009

Table of Contents

Chapter 1

"Lady Miyo! Lady Miyo!" The boy's voice rang through the grove of trees. He sounded angry, and a little scared.

A light smile crossed Miyo's lips. She ignored the voice and walked up the narrow game path through a stand of mixed oaks. The air was far cooler here than in the low-lying basin where her palace stood. Still, she had to wipe her brow, sweating from the steepness of the path. Her hand was sticky with the powder that coated her face, hiding her tattoo. A look in the bronze mirror hidden at her breast would not have revealed a pretty sight.

The keening of the cicadas felt loud enough to pierce her skull.

"Lady Miyo!"

The voice was closer now. The boy must be cutting straight across the thicket. The sword at his waist rustled the underbrush, then he burst onto the path beside Miyo, gangly legs struggling to keep pace with her.

Miyo threw the boy a sidelong glance and almost burst out laughing. His face looked as if he'd landed in a puddle. His hair was festooned with swatches of spiderweb. A potter after a hard day's work might have looked better.

1

Miyo finally paused. She turned, then gestured toward the boy's face. "Slow down, Kan. You'll spoil your good looks."

"Don't trouble yourself over me," he replied, catching his breath. His gaze traveled over her face. Eyebrows arched, he pushed Miyo's hand aside and touched her cheek. "My lady, your face looks even worse!"

"You needn't be so truthful."

"A person like you shouldn't... Now, please don't move." Miyo tried to turn away, but Kan held her arm and began busily applying powder to her face, as if she were an errant daughter. The work soothed him.

Kan was the only male permitted to touch Miyo. She would not have had it otherwise; yet that was probably because he was still just a boy, too young to bind up his hair. With Kan's motherly attentions complete, Miyo took her turn wiping his face. *Still just a sprig*, she thought.

By the time Miyo had finished carefully cleaning his face, the color had returned to Kan's round cheeks. He was at that age when the jaw starts filling out and the profile sharpens, but those large, sulky eyes were nothing like those of a grown man. Miyo felt safe with him. Someday this fourteen-year-old would be a strapping specimen even taller than she was, but for now he was in no danger of breaking hearts.

Miyo was a virgin—in fact, as well as name—and it seemed likely she would remain one for some time.

"Just how far do you intend to go?" Kan grumbled, brushing shards of rock from his bare soles. "We've already walked fifty *ri*. If we don't turn back now, we might not reach the palace before dark."

"Why go back? If it comes to it, we can stop near Ikaruga and wait the night out there."

"Please—don't tease me." Kan scowled. Teasing him was

precisely the point, and Miyo was poised to continue, but his next words stopped her.

"Think of Joh. She's so afraid when you are away."

Joh was Kan's sister. Plucked at random from the maids in the palace, she was compelled to stand in for the queen when Miyo was away. Of course, all she had to do was sit in the dim inner shrine, with no duties to speak of other than play the part, speak when spoken to, and be waited on hand and foot by Miyo's capable maidservants. Yet such was not a welcome duty for youngsters like Kan and Joh, bound to a life of service and unaccustomed to being served as Miyo was.

"You're right, Kan. It has been hard for her."

"Well, then—" *let's return*, he was about to say, but Miyo casually cut him off. "Yes. Let's keep going." She walked on. Kan brought up the rear with a sigh.

The mountain path quickly climbed higher. Here and there large boulders jutted through the moist black soil. Taller than the average male and toughened by her duties, Miyo clambered straight over them with little shortness of breath. Kan tried to scamper nimbly around them, but his meager diet betrayed him, and he quickly fell behind.

"Where," Kan gasped, out of breath, "are we going?" Miyo had planned a surprise, but this was beginning to seem slightly cruel.

"To see the ocean."

"The ocean!"

"You've never seen it, have you?" As Miyo spoke, they emerged onto the spine of the ridge. A fresh breeze hit their faces. Kan shielded his widening eyes from the glare and cried out in admiration.

The panorama before them stretched far to the west. A broad river ran north, along the foot of the mountains. At one point along its bank, an enormous host labored with digging tools, gouging the face of the plain. To the right, toward the north, stretched a lake surrounded by mud flats. The plain beyond the river was an endless carpet of paddy fields, verdant with rice seedlings. Farther out a harbor dotted with white sails, water shimmering in the sun.

The early summer sunlight flowed over the blue haze of the landscape. The scene was like nothing in the low-lying plain where they lived. There was the slightest whiff of ocean in the air. Kan filled his lungs with it.

"Is this what you came to see?" he asked.

"Yes. I heard you can see the ocean from Mount Shiki. Look there—the lower reaches of the Hatsuse River. It flows near the palace. Beyond is Lake Kusakae. On the canal from the lake to the sea is the harbor of Naniwa."

"Are they building something along the river?"

"They're straightening it. You gave my oracle to the ministers—the order to straighten the river's course to the sea. Whenever there's a heavy rain, floodwaters damage the crops. Have you forgotten?"

"Oh, that." Kan shook his head. Such matters no doubt held little meaning for him. He was merely a conduit of communication between Miyo and her ministers; the significance of her oracles was wholly beyond him.

Yet in a sense, for Miyo it was no different. It seemed passing strange to see this mass of people, moved by her divination to change the face of the land. This feeling only grew stronger as she spoke again of the sights below.

"See there? That wide avenue coming down from the north is the Shiha Harbor Road. The town at the end of it is Suminoé Harbor. And beyond that, the Chinu Sea."

"I see great ships. Enormous. Do they come from Wei?"

"Perhaps," said Miyo. Then it occurred to her that the ships might hail from somewhere else. "Or from Kushina or Akuso."

"Maybe they're from Kentak. Or Roma."

Miyo tried not to laugh. *Not likely*, she thought. *Innocent Kan thinks a ship can take you anywhere, but Kushina and Akuso are even farther than Wei, and they say Roma and Kentak are on the other side of the world, a voyage of several hundred days. Sea trade with those lands is decades in the future.*

Yet it was a fact that ships from these distant countries had reached the Land of Wa. Half the vessels sent on the return diplomatic mission were lost, but the rest survived to make it back, perhaps protected by the scapegoats they took with them on the voyage. They returned to Miyo's realm with astonishing articles of foreign culture from countries beyond the empires of China. Many more ships would surely ply those waters—someday.

"If we went with one of those ships, we could visit countries we've never seen," said Kan.

Was that what he really wanted? Or was it something that he thought could never really happen? With one eye on Kan's enraptured profile, Miyo sank deeper into thought. This world really was a mystery.

Her thoughts traveled back twenty-odd years, when chaos reigned the length and breadth of Wa. Wars over water and territory among the great clans—Nu, Toma, and the rest—had embroiled dozens of smaller chiefdoms. Countless people died, countless villages had been put to the torch.

Still, such terrible conflict could not drag on forever. There were men of compassion among the clans, men who knew Wa would be laid waste if the fighting did not stop. A ruler was raised over them all, the nations made peace, and since that day the Land of Wa had been free from strife. Relations were sometimes tense with the San'on lands, with Kunu and the other chiefdoms that stayed outside the union. But for the most part, Heaven and Earth were at peace, and an era of plenty was underway.

None of this would have been possible without the Laws of the Messenger.

The Laws were recorded on a single scroll handed down from a time lost to memory. Of the many chiefdoms of Wa, only Kunu did not possess a copy of the Laws. Their origin was unknown, but the meaning was plain. Calamity is part of the fabric of this world and is certain to come, but those who join hands and work together will stave off disaster. And in the end, a mighty host will come to deliver victory.

To Miyo, the Laws were little more than stale platitudes. For the clan leaders, they were sacred and inviolable, and the headmen were apt to invoke them in the most trifling of circumstances, for once invoked they must be obeyed. Had the Laws not commanded cooperation between the clans, the fighting would likely have gone on without end, no matter how great grew the weariness of the people.

Strange, too, was it that the Laws were known to each and every inhabitant of Wa. Stranger still, thought Miyo, was the fact that they were known in Wei and the other Chinese empires, as well as in Kushina, Kentak, and Maya.

It was said that seventy or eighty years had passed since the first ships from Kentak, piloted by red-skinned people over the vast ocean beyond the Chinu Sea, had reached Wa. At first, using gestures, they requested fresh water and an exchange of laws. When the leader of the small chiefdom where the visitors made landfall did as he was asked and showed them the Laws, he discovered that the visitor's own laws, written in their language on a sheet of animal hide, matched his scroll down to the smallest detail. The headman was astonished, but the red-skinned captain merely gave a knowing nod.

Exchanges progressed, and at each port the Kentak sailors

visited they demonstrated the universality of the Laws. It seemed that all peoples under Heaven were bound by the same obligation to join together and stave off disasters. Without this accident of history, collaboration among the chiefdoms of Wa might never have been possible. For Miyo, the Laws were platitudes, but their influence could not be denied. Because of the Laws, Miyo was forced to serve the state.

"Indeed," Miyo said to herself. She looked down at the rich fields and bustling seaports spread out before her. *What would this world have become without the Laws of the Messenger?* War without end, killing without limits, each individual cut off from all others.

Throughout the land, all agreed on their good fortune. But Miyo paid for it with her freedom.

She felt a wave of revulsion at the thought of her enormous power and absently took a step forward. Then she turned, her reverie broken by the sound of Kan's bronze sword leaving its sheathe.

"Lady Miyo—" His voice was charged with apprehension. "Lady Miyo, come back."

"What?"

"Your domain ends here. You are forbidden to leave it."

"Nonsense, the view is poor. See, beyond that tree…"

"Miyo!" He was pleading now, his voice rising almost to a scream. Miyo froze. She was fond of Kan, and he of her. She could not abandon him. They shared an affection for Kan's sister serving at the palace. Neither of them was ready to escape.

So this was it. Her bond to the state, to headmen, officials, ministers. Of all the shackles they had placed on her, this was by far the cruelest.

Miyo stepped back quietly. She turned and smiled. "Forgive me. Let's go home."

Kan's air of profound relief reminded Miyo how much she hated the state—and the Laws of the Messenger, bringer of peace to the world.

"We must hurry. Better to return to Ikaruga and take the post horses from there. But please step carefully," said Kan.

Miyo kept her eyes on his back as he strode ahead of her. She couldn't help wishing he were a little older. *If only we could run away together, escape the wiles of the state...*

Something shook the underbrush close by the path. The cicadas fell silent.

In one smooth motion, Kan drew his sword again. His stare bored into the thicket. Miyo stepped behind him and to one side, arming herself with an oak branch. It was less of a weapon than the sacred staff she used in divination rituals at the palace, but better than nothing.

Kan called out, "Who goes there?"

Wild dogs make no sound. If this were an ape, it would retreat. *No,* Miyo thought, *it must be a woodcutter. Or a hunter.* She hoped it was. Then there would be little to worry about. The common folk would not know her; she could easily talk her way out of things.

Bandits? Then they would be in real trouble.

Miyo swallowed. The hair on Kan's arms stood up. The thicket parted and a towering shape emerged as if from nowhere, its shadow falling over them.

At first they could not grasp what they were seeing.

The creature stood on two legs, like the bears that roamed the eastern lands. It was perhaps twice the height of a man. The two of them together could not have encircled its torso even if they'd clasped hands. Huge faceted eyes, insect eyes, twitched in their sockets, peering down at Miyo and Kan.

The creature was built like a bear, but everything else about it was unlike anything they had ever seen. The body was completely hairless, its hide red like a coating of rust. The way it leaned forward, long arms dangling, was more ape than bear. Here and there, whitish bones peeked through its coarse skin. The fingerless right arm was bludgeon-shaped. The left limb was like a scythe, yet sharper than any blade Miyo and Kan had ever seen. But they could not absorb all these details clearly. They were simply overwhelmed.

The creature's body gave off a pungent, smoldering smell. It eyed them intently and emitted a repulsive insect drone.

It is a law of nature—almost without exception—that the large prey on the small. Miyo and Kan knew this only too well. Deep in the mountains of this land were places where enormous creatures held sway, beyond the reach of men.

They were frozen with terror, struck dumb and drenched with sweat, their knees quivering. Except for a tiny boon of luck, they would have been taken where they stood. But luck did come, in the guise of a tiny deerfly. It flew, buzzing, landed on Miyo's ankle, sank its proboscis into her flesh, and began to feed. The stinging pain brought her to her senses.

"A mononoké!"

As she recovered her voice, her sense of danger reasserted itself. She slapped Kan's back with her open palm. Startled into awareness, the boy roared from the pit of his bowels and plunged forward.

"Eeeyaahhh!"

His sword, a green-black arc, struck the mononoké on the crown of its head. One multifaceted eye collapsed inward with a crumpling sound, but the monster showed no sign of pain. It raised its club arm high and brought it down with a dull hum. The club struck Kan's arm with brutal force, tossing him aside as if he were a puppy. He tumbled across the ground in a cloud of dirt. In an instant Miyo was at his side, stroking his battered arm. "Kan!"

He grunted in pain and winced as he got to his feet. "Not my sword arm," he muttered. He meant *I can keep fighting*, but that left arm was limp, dangling at his side. Very soon it would be swollen and black. "Go, Miyo."

"Don't talk like a fool."

"You are the fool. Hurry!"

The mononoké dropped its head and charged, the underbrush parting with a hissing sound. Its scythe arm was raised to strike. Miyo threw her arms around Kan and rolled violently to one side. The scythe boomed past them.

Miyo raised her head from the sticky grass to see a tree thicker than her thigh toppling, sliced through. Cold spread along her spine. The beast turned and moved in closer. The grass murmured. The immense creature's gliding, weightless silence was unnerving.

Will it eat us, like a bear? No—it has no mouth. It seeks no food. It hunts only to kill.

Without a sound, Kan leaped to his feet. His sword struck the monster's flank like a hornet's stinger. There was a cold, metallic clang and the weapon rebounded, shattering. Miyo took in Kan's dazed look and the sword's broken tip as it flew away, end over end. Was this monster made of stone? Of steel?

Despite her astonishment, Miyo maneuvered to one side of the beast. As it raised the scythe, she struck with all her strength, but the branch merely shivered from the impact. Then a tremendous blow knocked her flat.

"Kan!"

Kan threw himself atop Miyo, shielding her with his body. The scythe opened his back. To Miyo, everything seemed to be taking place in some other world.

"Kan..."

"Quickly..." The boy tried to speak.

"Kan?"

"Go quickly…" A whispered groan. Bright blood welled up from the gash, pooling on his back in a crimson lake. The mononoké emitted a creaking sound. It might be tiring, but it showed no signs of breaking off the attack. Again, it raised its club. Before it could strike, Miyo hoisted Kan's slender frame onto her back and fled, stumbling forward as she ran.

"You think I'd leave you?" she yelled.

She heard a series of sharp cracks, the mononoké raking the standing timber as it advanced. Its footfalls swept closer with horrifying speed. Miyo plunged forward, staggering, stumbling, slipping.

Something hissed close by her ear. Miyo crouched lower, to crawl, scrabbling on all fours, climbing the slope, her pulse hammering. She gasped for air and pitched forward, eating a mouthful of dirt. She felt the rush of air as giant legs planted themselves on either side of her.

Miyo could see the western ocean shining in the distance. She looked up at the belly of the beast as it stooped over her. *Strange*, she thought. *To die like this. We could have gone the other way, over the far side of the ridge.*

Was this retribution for daring to leave her realm?

A sudden sequence of huge booms split the sky over her head. The shockwave pressed her flat against the earth.

"Bolt fire ineffective. Target appears to have withdrawn voluntarily. No counters, traps, or criticals. I'd say this is a rather low-grade RET, a newborn Reaper."

"Spare me the commentary. Any nests in the area? What about FETs?"

Two voices—one female, one male—but Miyo understood nothing they said. Her terror was unabated. Whatever it was that had brought down that roar like thunder over her head, it could only be another mononoké.

She struggled with bleary eyes to peer around her. The

monster was gone. In its place stood a man, tall and power-fully built. He was arrayed like a soldier, encased in soot-blackened armor webbed with cracks. A helmet completely covered his head, its visor concealing his face. In his right hand he gripped an enormous sword. He was clearly the source of the male voice but was like no man Miyo had ever seen.

"Both humans are viable. The female has minor injuries. The male has lost a considerable amount of blood. Loss of consciousness in six minutes." Again the female voice, but no one was there. The soldier approached and spoke to Miyo.

"Let me help the boy."

Miyo could not understand him, but she knew he was no threat by the way he held his sword, low and casually. All she could think of was Kan. She eased him onto the ground. The horrible wound on his back seemed far beyond help, but she tore a strip from her hem and tried to bandage him.

"Subject may survive one hour if blood loss is halted. If he's to be left here, antibiotics are required."

The female voice. Miyo glanced up. To her amazement, the voice seemed to be coming from the sword—and the man looked to the sword as he answered.

"Later. What about FETs?"

"None detected, not even a comm net. This suggests that the RET has not been fully activated. Probably a stray," said the sword.

"It may be a stray, but it's also a threat. Location?"

"Thirty-five meters from your position and holding. O—look out!"

A log hurtled from the trees, striking the soldier like a battering ram and flinging him through the air. The sword flew out of his hand and plunged into the ground, inches from Miyo. The mononoké scudded out of the woods and onto the ridge. It pounced on the soldier.

"Sword!" As the soldier shouted, the monster's heavy club swung down. With astonishing speed the soldier sprang to his feet, out of harm's way. He touched his hip and a swarm of small stones flew at the beast and exploded in a flurry of detonations. The mononoké flinched for just a moment, then advanced as if it had hardly noticed. Swinging club, then scythe, then club again, it pressed the attack.

"Throw me, woman." Miyo was transfixed by the fighting, but when she heard the voice of the sword she wheeled in surprise. It spoke again.

"Throw me to him. *Now!*"

The blade was huge, gently curved. The spine was milky white, but the edge was transparent and shone with a blinding radiance. This was nothing like Kan's sword, neither in make nor material. And it spoke!

"Quickly, woman!"

"Give me Cutty!" As sword and soldier called out to Miyo in the same moment, she understood. She wrenched the sword from the soil, marveling at its unexpected weight, and took a running start before flinging it through the air. Turning through its arc, the sword plunged grip first toward the soldier, who sprang to catch it.

The blade flashed white.

The giant's upraised club arm dropped away like a stalk of grass beneath a razor. The swinging scythe shattered like glass. As the mononoké staggered, the sword swept across its belly. The soldier leaped atop the creature and hacked at the bug-like head, severing it from the body. Then he plunged the sword into the creature's neck and twisted it. "Burn!" he roared.

From the stump came a hissing sound like hot iron plunged in water, then a thin plume of smoke. The dismembered behemoth toppled backward as the soldier jumped down from it. The soldier stowed his sword in the sheath across his back and walked over to Miyo.

Surely this was some waking dream. How could Miyo have defeated such a being? She might have needed a hundred soldiers or more, and a stout fort. They might have lured it into a deep pit. That was the only defense she could imagine. Yet this man took mere seconds to cleave the horror into pieces. Miyo knew no other legend to match it, and so she knew him, the ancient sage whose word was proclaimed throughout Heaven and Earth. There could be no other answer.

"You are...the Messenger? Of the Laws?"

The soldier spoke over his shoulder. "Language."

"There seems to be some vowel shift relative to the root stream, but the language is still recognizable as archaic Japanese. Shall I translate?"

"Confirm the era and I'll do it myself. Chronocompass reads two, four, eight CE. Yours?"

"The same."

The soldier nodded and spoke to Miyo. "I am Messenger O. Do you understand?"

O. *The word for king,* Miyo thought. "I understand. You are Messenger...O."

"I bring tidings of war."

Miyo lifted the hand she'd been pressing against Kan's wound and bowed her head deeply. "Messenger O, I thank you. You have delivered us."

"Save it for later. Let's have a look at the boy."

Miyo wordlessly yielded her place beside Kan. The Messenger leaned over the boy and touched his wound. Miyo caught a glimpse of blood-soaked white muscle through a gap in the bandage and reflexively turned away. After a few moments she looked back. Her eyes widened when she saw that the gash had been closed by a thin film.

"His wound..." Miyo faltered.

"There's nothing I can do about the blood. He needs rest," said the Messenger.

"I have no words to thank you." Miyo knelt, touching her forehead to the ground. Her eyes brimmed with tears of relief, but in another part of her mind she was beginning to feel uneasy. How would her ministers react to the coming of the Messenger, creator of the Laws? No doubt she would have to perform a divination to determine whether this event was propitious or not. But would tortoise shell or deer bone divination be enough? For an event of such momentous importance, someone might demand a sacrifice divination—the beheading of a condemned prisoner, with the future gleaned in the splash of blood.

And Miyo would have to preside over the sacrifice. *There is no need to go that far*, she thought. Miyo wanted to avoid a sacrifice at all costs. The Messenger stood.

"Tell me, woman. Is this your country? Are you a slave?"

"No."

"An outsider? Do you know anyone living nearby? I need information on local geography and the state of affairs in this country. Do you also call this place Mount Shigi?" asked the Messenger.

"Shiki. I know no one near here."

"You must know the way down the mountain, at least. I need to find a village. Show me the way."

"Why?"

"I came to meet the ruler of this land. He must prepare for war."

Miyo looked up at him. The ruler? Did the Messenger say he had come to meet not officials of state but the nominal ruler? If so, there might be a way out—a way to force her ministers accept him. What she needed was to link this strange occurrence with everything she had learned over the years. It just might work. No—she was certain it would. After all, if this were a matter for divination, why had she not foreseen it?

"Messenger O." Miyo stood tall and looked straight into his eyes, so as not to be intimidated by his towering presence. "I am no foreigner. When I spoke before, I meant that I am not a slave."

"I see. A princess, then?"

"No. I rule."

Miyo wiped her cheeks with care, revealing the tattoo of the shaman. She opened her tunic, exposing one breast, and drew forth the palm-sized bronze mirror. Carried as proof of her identity, this was the first time she had actually used it. She drew herself up, as if pronouncing an oracle, and solemnly spoke the name she had been given by kings and ministers.

"I am Himiko, Ruler of Wa, Friend of Wei, Queen of the land of Yamatai."

•◆•

They waited until dusk to set out. In the early morning hours they reached the capital of Yamatai, on the plain of Makimuku. They had traveled under the cover of darkness so that no one would see the imposing visitor, but that was not the only reason for the secrecy. The Messenger had to be received at the palace in a fitting manner. It would not do for him to slink inside.

Miyo's plan was this: First, she would conduct a divination at her own initiative, proclaim the oracle, and dispatch a party to the mountains. There, as predicted, they would discover the Messenger. Perhaps they would see signs of his power in the mononoké's dismembered corpse. That way, the ministers would be unable to raise objections to receiving him. All in all, this was far better than telling them she had stumbled on the Messenger during the course of an outing.

So Miyo did not return directly to the palace but brought the Messenger to kinsmen of Kan on the outskirts of the capital. Kan's people received their unexpected visitors with astonishment, but when they saw Kan, borne on the Messenger's back and gravely wounded, they dropped everything to tend him. Miyo watched silently from a corner of the tiny pit-house as Kan's relatives boiled water, wiped the child clean, ground healing herbs, and applied a poultice to his injuries.

While they nursed Kan, his father and white-haired grandsire glanced frequently at the visitors. Miyo ignored them, pretending not to notice. But the Messenger—sitting hunched over in the confines of the tiny hut—seemed nervous. "Queen Himiko," he whispered.

"Miyo."

"Miyo. You rule this land, don't you? The court physicians, or your maidservants? Couldn't they just as easily—"

"The ruler of Wa does not leave her palace. The ruler does not leave, therefore neither do the court physicians."

"Of course...but can't you tell them the boy was attacked outside the palace?" He glanced at the old man, who was taking care not to look at them directly. "Can you trust these people?"

"Far better than my own ministers. We've known each other long, since I was a mere child." For a brief moment, Miyo's thoughts wandered back twenty years, to a time before the chiefdoms chose a shaman queen to rule over all. She had been the daughter of a village headman, covered with mud, playing hide and seek in the grass. Her family was very close to Kan's, and they had showered her with millet cakes and gifts of fruit.

Traces of that closeness endured, and when Miyo made one of her frequent visits, Kan's people received her warmly, without question. But now a barrier of reverence and fear divided them. Miyo was here not as friend, but as sovereign; now too there was the Messenger. Plainly this was someone extraordinary. And so as ever—if not so much as with her maidservants, who dared not even meet her gaze—Miyo was cut off from the warmth of human tenderness.

The firelight showed some color returning to Kan's pale face, where not long ago he had seemed to be at death's door. The Messenger turned to Miyo, who was staring fixedly ahead. "I think he's out of danger."

Miyo took the hint. She rose to her feet. "Let's go outside. It's too crowded here."

They stepped outside and crossed the moat that encircled the cluster of houses. The chorusing of frogs enveloped them. No star gleamed through the thin cloud cover. The grainy moon, almost full, cast a gentle glow over the paddy fields. The Messenger sat down on the embankment.

"Agriculture is far ahead of schedule," he said quietly. "You're diverting the Yamato River, aren't you? That wasn't supposed to happen till the Edo era."

"Eh-doh?"

"Far in the future. But this whole area—it's very impressive. You should only just be starting to carve cropland out of the silt. Overall, I'd say this is three centuries, in some ways, maybe thirteen hundred years ahead of the root chronology."

"I detected fore-and-aft rigged oceangoing vessels with keels in the harbor at Suminoé. The technology of seafaring is a millennium ahead of schedule." Miyo heard the sword's voice, but did not ask what it meant. Her lack of understanding frustrated her, but at the moment there was something she had to know.

"Messenger O, what did you mean about preparing for war?"

"Ah. That. Well, you must fight, or you will lose."

"Lose what?" asked Miyo.

"In the near term, your lives. Ultimately, your species."
The word of the Laws, thought Miyo. *Disaster is inevitable.
Join hands or die.* The Messenger turned to look at her.
"You don't believe me?"

"Who is the enemy?"

"They come from beyond this world. We call them ETs.
Like the one you saw today, but traveling in packs. What
you saw was real. So you must believe me."

"But everyone knows the mononoké are real," said
Miyo.

"Do they, now?"

"Many tales are told of them, in Wa and in the Chinese
empires. They are terribly strong. Merciless monsters, yet not
invincible, not like the spirits one can neither see nor hear.
We people survive only because we continue to slaughter
and vanquish them. But today was my first encounter with
one. The village headmen say a plague of the beasts happens
every few decades."

"They're right." The Messenger pounded a fist on
the flat of his hand. "Wonderful. Excellent. If people in
this era see things as you say, my task will be that
much easier. Sometimes all I have to do is mention the
creatures and people start making ready to flee. That's
not going to help. My message is this: the ETs must be
destroyed. Instead of fleeing in fear, we must annihilate
them."

"But why?" Miyo slowly ran her eyes over the soldier's
well-muscled body. "Did you not dispatch it with ease? Why
not do the same with the rest?"

"I could—fighting them individually. The one I killed was
a stray, separated from the pack. Probably from a colony
that arrived in ages past. What you saw today was nothing

compared to the terror of the horde. Don't you have records of anything like that?"

Miyo paused, then spoke. "Yes. They say the empire of the Hsiung-nu, in the far west of China, was destroyed by them. The Hsiung-nu joined forces with the surrounding kingdoms to stop a huge army of mononoké, but were wiped out. It seems our good relations with Wei, Kushina, and Roma came out of this. I never believed the story myself. So it was true after all."

"Very."

Miyo shuddered. An army of mononoké, strong enough to annihilate an empire? These were grim tidings indeed. "If these creatures are so frightful, I don't see that we have the strength to vanquish them."

"No, it's possible. They don't come in force initially. First they build small nests and build up their numbers. To find and destroy a nest before they've had a chance to multiply is within your capabilities. Cutty will handle search and location. I need you to mobilize your forces. But first you must learn to make steel. Bronze swords like the boy's won't do at all."

"We know about steel," Miyo said. The Messenger turned, his posture betraying disbelief. Miyo was glad of his astonishment, but checked herself from rejoicing. "Much steel was produced in Isumo, but it was forbidden. The mountains were left barren and rain washed down the poison. Is there a way to keep the poison from escaping?"

"No. Even if there were, we can't afford to worry about your environment. I want you to lift the ban and start producing as much as you can. Well, well. So you know about steel."

The Messenger nodded slowly, seemingly satisfied. Miyo suddenly sensed a deep fatigue behind his words and gestures, something she hadn't noticed by day. The weariness didn't seem physical—he'd carried Kan fifty *ri*, almost fourteen

Roman miles—and she'd had trouble just keeping up with him. As far as physical fatigue was concerned, she needed rest more than he did. No, this was something deeper, a weariness of the soul. On impulse, Miyo leaned toward him. "Don't you ever take off your helmet?"

"Of course."

The Messenger turned toward her, grasped his close-fitting, bell-shaped helmet with both hands and lifted it off. Miyo was astonished to see a wiry, masculine face covered with stubble, close-cropped hair the color of dry grass, deep-set eyes, and a prominent nose. As he peered at Miyo—she couldn't be certain in the darkness, but even his eyes seemed to be of some pale hue—the Messenger cocked his head amiably. "You don't seem surprised."

"I've seen foreigners before." But she struggled to conceal her surprise. Somehow, this was exactly how she thought he'd look. *He's exhausted.* His smile could not hide the shadow behind his sunken cheeks and the crooked line of his mouth. Even Miyo, with no experience of men, knew a single day of hardship could not cast such a deep shadow over one so strong.

"Where did you come from?" In spite of herself, Miyo felt a growing interest in this man. "What happened to you? You seem so…gaunt."

"Do I look that bad?" The Messenger seemed slightly surprised, but then he smiled. "Don't worry about me. You're the one who should be resting. Walking that far without rest is hard for a woman. You must be tired."

"Not at all. This day was easy compared to rituals at the palace."

"But you've had nothing all day except swamp water. At least get something to eat."

The Messenger's repeated urgings made Miyo suspect he was trying to change the subject. Perhaps he didn't care to have others nosing about in his affairs. But she was about to entrust her fate and that of her people to this man. She could not remain in the dark about him.

Suddenly the sword spoke quietly. "O, heads up."

In one movement he was standing, sword in hand, but after peering into the darkness he just as quickly relaxed. Miyo turned to see something atop a rock. Nearby, an old woman was sliding backward across the ground in an attitude of reverence. It was Kan's grandmother.

Miyo went to look. There was a tray with hot rice porridge and dried cakes, enough for two.

"Sustenance. Now we can talk a bit longer." Miyo brought the tray over. She watched the Messenger as she set out the plates. The cakes were made from dried dates, carefully set aside last autumn. Miyo tasted one. An inexpressibly delicious sweetness melted across her tongue.

The Messenger stared at the porridge a long time before taking a bowl in both hands and inhaling half the contents in one go. He sighed deeply. "My first food in twelve centuries."

Miyo paused. She returned the cake she'd been eating to its dish and silently passed him the entire tray. It was as she thought. This man had traveled here from some far country.

"Where did you come from?"

"Before this? I was on ops in the New Kingdom, in Egypt...no, I'd better start at the beginning." With no further hesitation, he began devouring the food. Then he glanced at Miyo. "You'd best keep this to yourself."

"I intend to."

"I come from a world 2,300 years in the future. But not your future. My journey spans many timestreams that are doomed to disappear."

Miyo held her breath and settled back to listen.

Chapter 2

"Wake up."

"Wake up."

"Wake up."

"—acknowledged. I am, awake. Initiating self-diagnostic sequence. Confirming self-recognition. I am Messenger Unit Eight Six Niner Niner Eight One, subunit of the Sandrocottos AI. I serve that the human species may survive."

"Permission to load functions. Select your work name from the knowledge base."

"My work name is selected. It is Orville."

"Orville, we assign you this body. Innervate and set Second Law to self-preservation."

"I understand."

Orville opened his eyes. He extended his awareness into the hardware that comprised his body and began taking inventory.

Implementation: cyborg, compound organic/synthetic. Length: 180 centimeters. Weight: 75 kilograms Terra Normal. Format: Homo, standard. Reproductive function: disabled. Growth function: disabled. Endurance/reflexes/

strength: hyperenhanced. Extranet links: enabled. Health status: optimal.

Readiness: 100 percent.

Orville locked his initial awareness values to Euthymic, calibrating his Self accordingly. Then he rose from his bed and inspected his environment.

A hospital room in soothing colors. Two white-uniformed operators were studying him intently. Orville sensed there was something significant about his being initialized in this environment instead of on a fabroom worktable. Not that they'd treat him as human, of course. But at least he'd experience far better handling than a nonsentient robot.

One of the walls was switched to view mode. Neptune loomed enormous, suspended in the blackness. Orville walked to the wall and looked down. The city below him was lit, not by the distant Sun, but by many intense luminosity sources suspended several hundred meters above the surface. Roads curved gently through thick forest cover. Tall, strongly built residences and buildings were visible among the trees. Automated vehicles ferried commuters in a smooth, unending stream. Humans in civilian clothes strolled here and there. In a large square, some sort of ball game was in progress.

The city seemed to have been designed for comfortable living. It looked neither like a metropolis with an exploding population nor like a bristling military base. But of course it was both.

"Welcome to Triton, Orville."

Orville turned. One of his youthful operators was smiling. With a blank, professional expression, the other operator brought Orville a robe and placed it on his naked body.

"How are you feeling? Any discomfort? Any nonspecific anxiety or hostility? Feelings of panic?"

"My condition is excellent. I am happy to be awake. I wish to fulfill my purpose."

"That's splendid," said the operator. "But we're in no hurry. We want you Messengers to get thoroughly acclimated to Triton. First, would you like to try eating? Of course, you don't require nutrients, but I'd like you to put your food privileges to good use."

"An excellent idea. I'm born, now for my first meal. Wait—it's not breast milk, is it?"

With a look of amusement, the young man gestured toward the exit. "You seem quite easy to communicate with. I'd like to join you. Order anything you wish—but I can't offer you breast milk."

And Orville's life began. Many other Messengers were awakened at the same time, and spent their first days being initiated into the mysteries of daily life. The expert AIs assigned to look after them were masters at socializing newly awakened cyborgs. Some Messengers, unable to tolerate being treated like children, soon transferred out of the facility. But Orville doggedly stuck with his operators. He sensed it might indeed be a problem if he put his clothes on backward or greeted someone from a distance of thirty meters, or for that matter three centimeters. So he learned to dress himself and to greet others from a distance of three meters; in the process he encountered his own levelheaded yet irrepressible nature. Before long he was ready to enter the world outside, the world of people.

He was assigned a place to live and personal property every bit as good as the average citizen. Triton was built for comfort—as much as its distance from the Sun allowed—and Orville fell in love with it. But the existence of this pleasant city was itself based on something far from pleasant. The decision to build on Triton was made in the shadow of extinction.

Sixty-two years ago, human life on Earth was annihilated.

•◆•

Triton Central Council, Sol System—this was Orville's outfit on humanity's principal stronghold. Three centuries before, when techniques of interplanetary communication and administration were perfected, some had predicted capital cities would cease to be necessary for centralized government. But the capitals survived; humans are political as well as social animals. Of course, the opposite urge—to avoid certain members of the community—was as strong as ever, and there were countless self-governing free cities scattered throughout the system, but only beyond the orbit of Jupiter.

As part of their training, Orville and his fellow Messengers were assembled at a facility run by the Central Council's Sol System Recovery Command. The human general standing before them wasn't recounting dry history. She was speaking of a tragedy that had struck her own family.

"We call the enemy ETs. At first it meant extraterrestrials, but once the fighting started, they were Enemies of Terra. After we lost Earth, they were simply Evil Things. We've attempted to end this war on thousands of separate occasions. We tried ceasefires. We tried negotiating. We tried surrendering. Tried to expel them. Tried to quarantine them. Nothing worked.

"Forty-six years ago, we tried extermination. At first it seemed to be working. Our projections had Sol System liberated within a decade. Then they attacked with weapons of mass destruction, including a giant reflector in geosynchronous orbit above Earth. Except for some of the archaebacteria, the biosphere perished. We spent six months reterraforming our home planet, but it looked like we'd need three centuries to reestablish the biosphere out of our DNA archives. Even then, we could only have recovered five percent of species. We managed to lose in a generation what it took our planet four billion years to create.

"We know a few things about these ETs. They are self-replicating fighting units. In terms of technical sophistication, they're somewhat ahead of us. Their goal is the extermination of our species. For all we know, they may even be a product of human intelligence. But our senior analysts agree they're probably from outside our system, because they've mounted attacks on colonies orbiting stars in this neighborhood. We're not sure why, but they also attacked an automated observation station near Teegarden's Star. That kind of offensive reach is beyond the capabilities of any human settlement in the Local Group.

"Because we received warning in time, we were able to nip these attacks in the bud. Still, we don't know anything about their origins—where they're based, habitat and culture, the motivation for these attacks. Nothing."

The general was middle-aged. Her detached delivery belied the fact that, as Orville and the others already knew, she had lost her husband and five members of her family in this war. Her loss fueled the single-mindedness that propelled her to her present rank.

"First infiltration was on Venus, using covert spore insertion. After replicating and building up their strength, they initiated hostilities by constructing a disk that blocked all light from the Sun. The disk was half a million kilometers in diameter and completely deprived Earth of sunlight for three years. Impact on the biosphere and food production was staggering. But the disk was also a tactical diversion aimed at channeling our defensive efforts. We put most of our resources into reinforcing our off-world units, and when we finally deployed against the disk, the enemy landed in force on Earth. Within a week, they'd spawned four hundred thousand anthills. This completely disrupted our bases and command-and-control networks, which in turn prevented us from repelling attacks from their remaining forces in space.

"By the war's fifth year, it was all over for Earth. In year six Mars fell. Year eight, we lost the asteroid belt. By year ten they had advanced as far as Jupiter. That was the year our species decided to withdraw to a new defensive perimeter far from Sol, with Neptune as the hub. We called for assistance from the exoplanet colonies and hunkered down for a war of attrition.

"At this point, we were down to seven percent of our pre-war population. But the enemy apparently depends on solar energy—specifically, they appear to distribute solar power by means of laser-modulated transmission—and they failed to mount major attacks against the outer planets, where the Sun's energy is greatly attenuated. This gave our species hope for recovery. It was no mean feat to produce antimatter without solar energy, but forty years of work have brought us this far. And now, humanity is on the offensive. The history of our offensive, and our victories, will surely be written someday. But not by me." The general paused a moment before continuing. Her detached tone was replaced by something approaching emotion.

"The future of this struggle is in your hands. It is no longer for humanity to fight these battles, nor to tell how they were won. All we can do is support you. So I close with this: go forth to victory. Dismissed."

For Orville, the general's final words were more than a military directive. They resonated with humanity's experience and resolve. Now the Messengers would be the bearers of that resolve, if necessary transmitting it to others.

In point of fact, the Messengers did not need to hear the general's speech. Messenger AIs were equipped with the fruit of nearly all of mankind's intellectual achievements, backed by the Sandrocottos AI, Supreme Commander of the Sol System Recovery Force. As Messengers, they knew more about the origins of this war than any human. The time they spent living as humans prior to deployment was not to teach them what humans knew. It was designed to instill in them human sensibilities, to encourage them to ponder the significance of humanity, of society, and finally, of their own identity.

As highly advanced intelligent organisms, the Messengers were far more than machines designed for service. They were capable of harboring profound doubts regarding themselves and the world, and many of them did. If Messengers were to have the ability to question the basis of a given action, they had to be endowed with a self capable of providing an answer. Their father Sandrocottos did not tell them who they were, nor did he think this was something that could be taught. The self is the history each individual makes through living life. Knowing this, Sandrocottos gave them a single directive: discover for yourselves what you fight to defend.

Orville and his kind were produced by different designers and builders in batches of several hundred to several thousand units; Messengers were endowed with varied temperaments from the outset. Based on its temperament, each Messenger chose a personal path for establishing a self. One Messenger might devote itself to the study of science, seeking mankind's essence through the accumulation of knowledge. Another might delve into religion, seeking ultimate value in its manifold patterns and multiple ways of interpreting the universe. One might seek to understand art in its widest sense; another might narrow his focus to the development of a single creative field such as literature or music.

But most Messengers made an effort, above all else, to venture out into the world—to observe its sights, experience its sounds and smells, converse with its people. By exploring the fullest potential of the complex organic machine interfaces that were their bodies, they were able to acquire knowledge through the broadest number of pathways. These pathways formed the basis for memory, which is why more than half of all Messengers were assigned physical bodies. It was hoped the precious memories created by going out into human society would sustain them during the long journey that lay ahead.

The Messengers came to see Triton as a wonderful place. Resurgent humanity was done biding its time, and Triton was the focus of that resurgence. The city overflowed with passion and vigor, wealth and energy. And it was there on Triton that Orville found his reason for living—the deathless memories of his days and nights with Sayaka.

●◆●

He found her working at a window in the Defense Force Supply Section. It was an odd place for an encounter. Even stranger was her behavior: she had one foot up on the counter and was emptying a mug of coffee over the head of a requisitioner. That was Orville's first glimpse of Sayaka.

This was somewhat unusual behavior for a clerk in a military installation—in fact, he had seen nothing to match it anywhere on Triton—so Orville approached her. "What are you doing?"

"What was that?" Her hair, the color of burnished gold, was pulled back tightly and piled on her head. A tie encircled her throat, her suit was immaculate. Nothing in her appearance would have predicted what she'd just done. Not only did she take the trouble to pour the last drop of coffee onto the head of her dazed customer, she balanced the empty cup on his head.

"This is my job. I distribute supplies to the right people."

"I've never seen it done that way," said Orville.

"Excuse me. What I *meant* was, I make sure supplies don't go to the *wrong* people."

"Ah, I see." Orville paused for the two milliseconds needed to query the Supply Section AI about its responsibilities and work practices. The AI responded that it handled over 90 percent of all hardware/software aspects of matériel distribution to Defense Force units, but special cases were left to humans. Of course, the AI was equipped with the expertise to manage human organizations, and it understood that extralegal or irregular procedures were sometimes required. Special cases were the task of this human-staffed department.

In other words, thought Orville, *this is the administrative back door to the Supply Section.* Still, he was unable to find anything in the normal procedures to account for the woman's actions, so he decided to investigate further. "Do the wrong people come here?"

"I've got one in front of me," she answered. "Little cheat, he's trying to snitch some parts for an obsolete terrestrial loader. So he can sell them, naturally."

His cover blown to everyone in the office, the man clucked his tongue with contempt and departed, the cup falling from his head. The woman finally took her foot off the counter. A cleaning bot started working on the mess. The next customer fearfully retreated to a different window.

The woman looked at Orville. "What are you looking at? This is my job. I decide who doesn't get loader parts, or half-spoiled food from the warehouse, or surplus strategic warheads. I'm sick of these combat shirkers coming in trying to rip us off."

"How do you decide who's legitimate?" Orville asked.

"I look at their face." The other clerks had been struggling not to laugh. Now they couldn't help it. Judging from their reaction, Orville concluded that the woman must be like this all the time, and it was encouraged. It seemed odd that the otherwise meticulous support AI took no action while she flagrantly abused her authority.

The woman seemed to read Orville's thoughts. "So? What do you want? Doesn't look like you're here to requisition something. Just dropped by to pay your respects? Or are you here to rate our performance?"

"I am a Messenger AI." Orville had already decided to ignore the way business was conducted in this place. Requisitioners and supply clerks glanced at him with mild surprise. The woman furrowed her brow, put a slender finger alongside her temple and pondered.

"In that case, I'll do the best I can," she said with some discomfort. "I know what Messengers do. But what do you need? We've got everything from main battle weapons to bathroom fixtures, but it's all obsolete junk."

"I just want to observe you for a while," Orville replied.

"Ob-*serve* me?" Her mouth fell open. Everything she did was exaggerated. Orville nodded.

"I'm not here to requisition anything. This is my free time. I find you interesting."

"But...why here? You're an AI."

"An embodied AI, created by Sandrocottos. My perception of the world is mediated by this body. I'm interested in you, here and now. This is me speaking, not some giant processor farm in a basement. Can I sit over there for a while?"

The woman stared down at the counter, muttering something unintelligible. Finally she looked up, blushing faintly, and smiled. "It's fine with me, if you don't mind watching me pour coffee on people I don't like."

"That's up to you."

The woman suddenly spun round and yelled at her colleagues, who were fighting back laughter. "What should I do? We've never had one of these elite types in here before."

Orville was somewhat taken aback to be referred to as elite. Maybe it was just Central Council publicity at work, but the Messengers weren't exactly dashing heroes who'd volunteered for this dangerous mission.

For the rest of the day, Orville watched as the woman devoted her attention to dealing with one applicant after another. She didn't pour coffee on anyone else, but she gave each applicant a merciless tongue lashing, from suspicious-looking, washed-up paramilitary types to Defense Force officers who had clearly chosen the wrong profession.

When she finished work, Orville invited her to dinner. At this point, he was mainly interested in her personality as an unusual example of bureaucratic culture. When she had changed and emerged from the building—her hair still tightly pulled back and piled on her head, but her tie loosened and her makeup refreshed—his interest moved in a slightly different direction.

Orville renewed his focus on her appearance. She was perhaps three centimeters taller than average. Not slender exactly. Not voluptuous either, but strong and lithe. She was young, maybe thirty or so. With average human lifespan over 140 years, there were many options for looking half one's age, including body renewal. But she looked like the real thing. Her skin was thick and lustrous.

The woman looked at Orville and narrowed her large, plum-colored eyes. "I don't know your name yet."

"Orville. 'Messenger Orville' is enough to contact me anywhere."

"Sayaka Kayaniskaya."

"That's a Russian name, out of the Valles Marineris. From the time of the Euroforce incursion," said Orville.

"You AIs know everything. But my mother's side of the

family is Asian." She whistled lightly and expressed a pref-
erence for spicy food. Orville retrieved the names of four
restaurants. The verdict: Sino-Spanish.

"So, you want to know why I'm so hard on people at
Supply?" To the surprise of neither, the debate was in progress before the aperitifs arrived. Given the relationship, there
was no particular need for diplomacy.

"I told you. I don't like them. Of course it's not personal.
As I said, as you saw, you can't use logic with these types.
They come to my window because logic won't get them past
the AI. So the first thing I say to every one of them is No."

"I understand the strategy. But some of them must be
legitimate," said Orville.

"They're all legitimate, as far as data and paperwork go.
But treat them like dirt and give them the cold shoulder?
Pretty soon you'll find out what they're really up to. You
can tell the ones who really need supplies. Insult them or
pour coffee on them, they'll stand their ground. The ones
who are in it for themselves won't go that far. Their goal
is to avoid attracting attention. But the ones willing to do
anything for the operation—or their people!—they don't
care if they cause a scene, or if somebody sends a report
upstairs. When I sense that, I give in. Sounds simpleminded,
but I've never read one of them wrong so far."

"But what's the basis for your judgment?" Orville persisted. "Should you help people willing to do anything for
a misguided operation? Or scoundrels who'll do anything
to get the goods so they can sell them? Frankly, I don't see
the connection between passion and probity."

"Well, I guess there might be some really passionate bad
apples."

After several courses, during which they seemed to be
groping for words, Sayaka's chopsticks paused in midair.
"I guess I'm talking about devotion," she ventured quietly

and shrugged, half expecting Orville to laugh at her old-fashioned sentiment. Instead, he was surprised.

"Devotion? To the military? Where do people get it?"

"I'm not talking about the Defense Force. They're just a tool to protect society, yes? I meant something bigger... devotion to humanity. Do you understand? *Humanity*."

Orville thought carefully about what she might mean by emphasizing that word. "You think highly of people who are devoted to humanity."

"Right." Sayaka gazed at him. Her amethyst eyes were shining with curiosity. Orville sensed this was an important test. Her opinion of him hung in the balance.

On the face of it, what she was describing was identical to his prime directive. But Sayaka was human. She couldn't possibly have the same sense of purpose as an AI. Three, maybe four decades of life experience—Orville hadn't reviewed all her personnel files, so as to have a more "human" perspective on his date—had led her to this conclusion. But after just a few hours with her, Orville was in no position to guess what she might mean.

He returned her steady gaze and said the only thing he could say. "I'm not sure I understand what you mean."

"What? Oh." Her tired laugh carried a hint of scorn. "Not your topic, is it? Well, I guess it's not a subject for the table anyway."

"That's not what I meant."

"Don't sweat it. Let's concentrate on the food. Ah, here come the Valencia crabs."

The conversation lost its rhythm. They fell silent. Finally Sayaka changed her tone and began expounding on the relationship between the spiciness of each region's traditional cuisine and their distance from the Sun. But by the time dessert arrived, the conversation was still dragging. They finished the meal and parted with no talk of meeting again.

Over the next two weeks, Orville made more new contacts, men and women both, than a normal human could count. Conversations never lagged, because he never felt the need to think deeply about what was said. Most of the talk revolved around the conflict with the ETs. As an AI, Orville had that sort of information at his fingertips. But when he was alone, he couldn't stop wondering how a delicacy like Valencia crabs could have seemed so tasteless. What had Sayaka meant by "humanity"? Was it the same humanity he was sworn to protect? Perhaps there was some facet of meaning he still did not grasp.

•◆•

One day Alexandr, another Messenger, took Orville to visit a decommissioned ship docked in the depressurized zone outside the city. Alexandr brought along a little girl named Shumina, who had asked him to help her retrieve some books.

"It's a library ship," enthused Alexandr. "They've got hundreds of thousands of volumes dating to the twenty-first century and even earlier. Can you believe it? Books made of paper. It's astounding that they survived all the fighting."

"Are you sure you needed me to come along?"

"Now don't say that, Orville. Books are very heavy, you know. We'll need help finding them and carrying them. We definitely need you here. Right, Shumina?"

"I wouldn't have minded just the two of us." The coffee-colored little girl giggled. Alexandr, who dwarfed her in size, blushed.

Shumina's goal was to become a children's writer. Alexandr had met her through a literary circle. Orville wanted to leave them and go back to the city immediately, but Alexandr begged Orville over his comm link not to go, and he reluctantly agreed.

When they arrived at the ship, they discovered it crammed with books stored in a protective vacuum. It wasn't exactly a friendly environment for humans, but with their enhanced physiology Orville and Alexandr made do with simple breathing gear and located Shumina's ancient children's books. Phase one of their mission accomplished, Alexandr and Shumina huddled together, absorbed in deciding which books to take back with them. With little to do, Orville set off for a walk around the ship.

Paper books. Brittle, awkward, unbelievably low-density databases. Yellowing hunks of fiber piled up like relics in airless or dusty rooms. In fact, they really were relics. The ship's contents were all that remained of the ancient British Library collection. Alexandr was drawn to such relics and so was probably drawn to humans with a fondness for such things. That at least was not difficult to understand. But Orville found it hard to share his enthusiasm. Books, and the wisdom they held, were nothing more than samples of humanity's values. Somehow, trying to understand humanity through a mass of samples was not quite enough for Orville.

Lost in thought, he was walking along a dimly lit corridor inside the ship's hull when he sensed a human presence ahead. Someone was transferring books from a bank of shelves to a cargo loader. Whoever it was seemed to be in a hurry. Instead of placing the books in the loader one by one, he was sweeping entire shelves clean—certainly not the best way to handle priceless relics. Then a shout came from somewhere behind Orville.

"You there! Hit the deck!"

The next instant, Orville found himself in the middle of a firefight. Shots came from behind; the man ahead returned fire. The air around Orville seethed with flying metal.

Again, the voice behind him: "Duck, you idiot! Want to get arrested too?"

Orville did not duck. Judging from the sonic signature of the bullets, the shooter behind him was using nonlethal rounds. He engaged his battle capabilities and broke into a run, covering the fifty yards to his target faster than any human sprinter, and had the man down and pinned to the floor before he could escape.

The firing behind him stopped. Footsteps approached. Orville turned to see the surprised face of Sayaka Kayaniskaya.

"You? But…why?"

"As a Messenger, I am of course a military weapon," answered Orville.

"No, I mean, why are you here?"

"Just minor business, I suppose. I was brought here by friends who are avid readers."

Sayaka was wearing light battle armor, with a gun and restraint gear. Orville turned the suspect on the floor over to her. "You're the one who's hard to understand," he continued.

"How so? Junk vessels like this are under Supply Section jurisdiction. I headed here the instant I heard a theft was in progress."

"Junk?"

"Yes, including the cargo. I mean, sure, it's pretty valuable junk. One of these could buy you your own frozen asteroid. Yeah, I know what they're worth."

Orville looked down at the bullet-riddled cardboard covers of the books. He had a different reaction, but he kept it to himself. "By the way, I guess book thieves like this aren't included in the 'humanity' you talked about." He glanced down at the thief.

"What 'humanity'?" Dubious, Sayaka's eyebrows narrowed.

Orville felt himself losing heart. "The humanity you wanted people to be loyal to," he persisted.

Sayaka's look of bewilderment slowly changed to one of surprise. "Oh, *that*? Are you still thinking about that?"

"I haven't been able to stop since I heard you say it," said Orville.

"All this time? But you said you didn't understand."

"That's what kept me thinking. It's something that ties in with my biggest doubts. It wouldn't have been right for me to just toss off an answer," Orville said.

"But, but then why didn't you just *say* that?" At that moment the thief gave a sharp tug, nearly pulling Sayaka off her feet. "Look, I better turn this perp over to the police."

"I already notified them. They should be here in five or six minutes. Better be careful, your suspect's got a laser knife."

Orville reached out and gripped the man's neck and right arm. A knife fell from his sleeve and clattered to the floor. The thief sat down, seemingly resigned to his fate. Sayaka blinked in amazement. Finally she regained her composure and shook her head. "Thanks. If he'd opened me up with that, I'd have a bit of a problem."

"More than a bit of a problem for me," Orville said.

"Really?" A smile flashed in her large eyes. Orville noted this and pressed on.

"I recognized your voice. That's why I didn't duck," he said.

"But what if I'd hit you? That really would've been a problem," Sayaka said. Orville smiled.

• ◆ •

Their second dinner took place in a steamboat stew restaurant. The conversation—and their chopsticks—never faltered. What were Messengers, exactly? What did they do? What did they think about? Orville answered all her questions, at least those he was at liberty to answer. Their mission was to help mankind by spreading word of the danger posed by ETs. Once deployed, they were to use all their capabilities to support the fight against the enemy. This directive was in their minds at all times.

But once the pot was cleared away, Sayaka's bright eyes were beginning to show the effects of alcohol. "Come on, let's forget all these,"—the mood changed—"these *generalities*," she murmured. "What are *you* like?"

Orville chose his words carefully. The conversation had turned serious. "I have no second thoughts about being sent into battle. No fears, no doubts. I feel no mercy toward the enemy. I seek no reward or compensation. But having said that, I have no intention of simply following orders. I want to know the reasons behind everything."

"Did you think you'd find them by falling in love?"

"Some Messengers do. Not me. Protecting those near you, protecting your friends, protecting Triton, human civilization—I can't be satisfied with that alone. Why should I actually do any of those things?" said Orville.

"I think the answer to that is, you'll never find the answer. I mean, probably. Soldiers have been asking themselves that question ever since there were soldiers."

"But I thought you knew," he replied.

"Even I can't answer that one."

Sayaka's casual shrug put an edge into Orville's voice. "You said you cared about people who were devoted to humanity."

"I did indeed. But, you know, other people's concept of humanity is something I can't know. I don't see how I could. There must be lots of different dimensions to that understanding. Someone might protect their superior officer with an escort robot. Someone else might distribute surplus food to war orphans or support logistics by running supplies along the main space routes with surplus ships. Anybody on the receiving end of that kind of help is going to see it as service to humanity.

"Then there are other kinds of people. Knowingly or unknowingly, it doesn't really matter, they pursue what benefits them regardless of the big picture. What I'm saying is, that's the kind of thing I hate. But you know what?"

Sayaka saw Orville frowning. Her own smile grew warmer. She drew her face close to his. "I didn't tell you before, but all this isn't really what's on my mind."

"What do you mean?"

"I'm sick of always having to think I'm on the straight and narrow to some distant ideal. It's dangerous, you know? So I'm taking a more relaxed view. Everything is to end the war." She laughed smugly and merrily emptied her glass. "That's right. War is just a process. Dressing people down and yelling at them? That's just till all this is over. After that, who cares? I'll watch while people do as they please, regulations be damned."

Orville stared at her, forgetting even to reply. He admired her without rancor. From an official standpoint she was spouting antiwar sentiment, far beyond anything Orville might have ever entertained. To call the war nothing more than a process to be tolerated when the survival of the species hung in the balance? That was beyond belief. Yet at the same time, Orville felt a strong surge of emotion, a sense that this way of thinking was something he needed to learn from.

That day marked the real beginning of their relationship. The more Orville learned about Sayaka, the stranger she seemed. It was like being with a kaleidoscope. She had an amazing network of contacts—not only workmates and the paramilitary types who came to the Supply Section, but people throughout the Defense Force Command, in the bureaucracy and in corporations, in the commercial district near her office and study circles and the places where she socialized; everywhere she went, she laughed, flared with anger, and wept the tears of others. There were always new facets of her personality on display. She could fill any room with her presence—she was frighteningly intelligent, with no reserve, no hesitation whatsoever.

Within minutes, she could enter seamlessly into any discussion. In conversations with many people, she could skillfully home in on a comment about to be lost in the chatter, skillfully guiding everyone's attention toward it. Self-satisfied braggarts felt her biting sarcasm, but she fiercely defended anyone on the receiving end of unfair criticism. When asked her opinion, she responded with constructive, insightful, considered advice. She was also a skilled listener. If necessary, she could share long silences with friends of few words. Even in the twenty-sixth century, the old traditions of female shyness and diffidence remained alive and well, but Sayaka seemed to be from another era entirely.

Orville began accompanying her everywhere, finding easy acceptance among her friends. He became skilled at poking fun at himself, putting people at ease. He learned firsthand that an AI's unlimited knowledge was sometimes of no use in relating to humans. Sayaka's preferred companions were, without exception, brilliant, masters of the witty comeback. A head stuffed with knowledge, even an AI's, counted for little with them. What really mattered was whether you knew your limitations and sought out those who had what you lacked. On this point, Orville was acutely self-aware, which enabled him to behave as a modest fool rather than as a conceited know-it-all.

But then something made him feel profoundly stupid, something that was not the fruit of his self-awareness. This was when Sayaka's friends asked him whether or not she let her hair down before bed.

For some reason Sayaka nearly always wore her hair up, whether the occasion was formal or relaxed. In a crowd, her striking combination of slender build and hair piled high, like an ancient warrior's helmet, made her conspicuous. But Orville knew that was not the gist of the question. People wanted to know what kind of relationship they had. After hearing the question two or three times the subtext was obvious even to him.

Of course, there was no law forbidding love between an AI and a human. The era when that had been considered problematic was more than three centuries past. And Sayaka made no distinction between AIs and humans. As far as she was concerned, it wasn't an issue.

Oddly enough, around the same time Orville began to ponder this, Sayaka's attitude changed. Where previously she had always been completely open and frank with him, she now became guarded. On two or three occasions, she had invited Orville to her house for dinner; then the invitations stopped. She avoided discussing humanity or what was worth defending. Instead, she talked only about people they knew, food, the latest trends, and other trivia.

At this point the average male would have begun to worry that the woman's interest might be waning, but unfortunately Orville was an AI with a heightened self-awareness. Even when he did not wish it, he was aware of Sayaka's pulse and thermal signature. He understood that far from ignoring him, she was harboring a special interest toward him.

In other words, she was in a quandary, and this posed a major problem. For more than two weeks after he first became aware of Sayaka's dilemma, Orville deliberated carefully. The problem, ironically, was his own feelings. Orville did not possess that mixture of vulgarity and pretension that drives human males to baldly approach females. On the other hand, he faced a very practical problem. Was it possible for him to love a woman? Were his feelings something he could trust?

Finally, the inevitable happened and Orville was forced to take action. One evening, he was at a bar with a new circle of friends. A young fleet officer—a man liked by all, including Orville—asked him more than half seriously, "Do you know whether Sayaka is seeing anyone?"

Orville was confused by the wave of emotion that rose up inside him. But before pausing to confirm what it was, he answered the question. "She isn't seeing anyone, as far as I know."

"Really? Great, thanks." The officer rose from his chair with a look of determination and headed for the table where Sayaka was chatting lightheartedly with friends. Only then did Orville recognize the source of his agitation.

It was jealousy. He could feel actual jealousy. This astonished him, but it delighted him even more. He hadn't expected to discover it this way, yet it confirmed his feelings for Sayaka. But this was no time for celebration; the officer had already wormed his way into the conversation and was casting frequent glances at her. The moment of truth would be along soon enough. No, there it was—the officer had requested the pleasure of her company, probably over at the long bar, and was already rising from his chair. Orville stood up.

When he reached the table, everyone turned to look at him. Sayaka, hand in hand with the now standing officer, was rising from her chair. She had just drawn a wry laugh from him, probably thanks to some cutting remark of hers, but she didn't seem to be refusing him either. When she saw Orville, her face froze along with her body, half out of the chair.

One of the group motioned with his glass for Orville to

join them. "Hey, Orville. Good timing. We've got a vacancy. Have a seat."

"Thanks, not right now. Sayaka, I need to talk to you," said Orville.

"Gosh, I'm sorry. I'm busy just now. Later, possibly—"

"It won't keep. It's probably the same thing he wants to tell you." Orville gulped and prepared to deliver his message, but Sayaka sensed what was coming and held up her hand.

"Wait. All right, Orville. Let's go over there. Next time, Yansen."

While the stymied officer struggled for something to say, Sayaka lowered her eyes, slipped past him, and went to the bar, Orville in tow. As soon as they sat down, she emptied her glass and stared straight ahead.

"All right, you first. I might be making the wrong assumption."

"You probably aren't. I want a relationship with you. As a man," said Orville.

"So I thought. Why the timing? Worried he'd beat you to the finish line?" she asked.

"Partly that, but I've been thinking about it for a long time. And so have you." Orville waited for her answer. He was not optimistic. If Sayaka were inclined to accept him, her slender eyebrows would not be almost touching now. Still, he couldn't help but be struck by her profile in the dim light of the bar. She was beautiful. Tightly pulled back, her hairline curved across her forehead like a glowing copper comb. The gently sloping line of her bare shoulders, the angled wrist holding her glass—she was more than just lovely form. Sayaka was delight. No human artifice could replicate it. This manifestation of decades of movement, animated by the mysteries of thought and experience, was something only humans possessed.

"You'll go." Her voice was a hoarse whisper. "You can't stay with me. You'll be deployed, that's for sure. How can you talk like this?"

"Is it wrong?"

"It's awful. Don't you think?"

"No, I don't," said Orville. "If it were, there'd be no point to love. This isn't like you. Are you so afraid of the future?"

"Of course I'm afraid!" She was staring at him now. Her amethyst eyes flashed with anger. "I've always tried to live with an eye on the future. How wonderful things will be when this war is over. Even with everything coming at us, military service and everything else, I thought things would just get better and better the more time passed. But if I fall in love with a Messenger, it'll all be for nothing."

"Is that what's been worrying you?" said Orville.

"You knew?"

"I know how to look. Maybe women have suffered the same kind of anxiety since the beginning. But if you care about me, try to understand how I feel. We Messengers don't even have a future to dream about."

"Orville..." Sayaka's eyes filled with tears. In a distant corner of his heart, Orville tasted bitterness. The logic of seduction that he was deploying to such effect was not his. It was the logic of the designers who made him. It was agonizing to realize he was simply fulfilling that design. But the desire he felt for Sayaka was real. Of that he was certain.

"If you feel anything at all for me, let me share your suffering. And of course, your joy," he said.

With a tearful smile, Sayaka dried her eyes and murmured, "'In sickness and in health.' How long has it been since anyone said that?"

She filled two glasses with wine and pushed one toward Orville. Her makeup was streaked with tears, but her smile was open and warm. She lifted her glass high. "All right. I'll be your lover. We'll share the good and the bad, fifty-fifty. But...let's make it fun."

"Cheers," said Orville.

The clink of their glasses rose above the din of the bar.

●━●

For the next four months, Orville loved a human female. Their days together were full of contentment—in the city, together at home, sometimes in a shuttle they'd take into orbit when they both had time. It was also a heady time for humanity, a golden age of the counteroffensive. Each day brought news of another ET nest destroyed, another colony reclaimed. Everyone threw their hearts into the work, every production facility ran flat out. The birthrate skyrocketed. Nurseries and schools rose one after another.

Orville and Sayaka exchanged wry smiles whenever conversation turned to the merits of doing one's bit for population growth. Messengers lacked the ability to reproduce. Even if Orville were fully functional, as it were, Sayaka's position (officially, at least) was that she had no time to bear a child, yet. But to close friends she half-joked, "You don't have to look nine months into the future to have fun in bed."

Though Orville never mentioned it to Sayaka, fertility was a topic of debate even among other Messengers. Opinion ran the gamut. Some wanted the ability to reproduce, some said it was not critical, others thought it should be forbidden. Alexandr believed in platonic relationships and emphasized the tie between soulmates. But when he dragged the concept of Original Sin into the discussion, Orville gave him a friendly warning: "No one doubts the nature of your relationship with Shumina. Just leave it at that."

On this point, Sandrocottos was unyielding. The ability

to reproduce sexually was the critical distinction between humans and AIs. It was a line that must not be crossed.

The importance of leaving descendants often came up when Orville and Sayaka discussed the value of resurgent humanity. For Sayaka, humanity meant not only the several hundred million people alive today. It meant a vast continuity, flowing from the past into the future—an ocean of more than five hundred billion individual lives. Orville liked that majestic image.

Sayaka had been born aboard Pluto Convoy, at the height of humanity's withdrawal to the far reaches of the solar system. Her mother had died in combat when Sayaka was small, and so she was raised by her historian father. As she moved with him from base to base, she developed an understanding of the flow of people and goods. When she reached adulthood and began searching for work, she realized her place was in the Supply Section.

By nature, Sayaka yearned for a return to something bigger than just community. Orville surmised that this desire had crystallized when she was a young girl. She was inclined to agree. That, she said, was why it was important to hold on to that idea from her childhood and turn it into something nobler, something bigger.

"These are strange days. A person can give their all to society, without a trace of misgiving." Sayaka sprawled languidly across her bed beneath the skylight. "No worries about being duped into serving tyranny or corruption. The results, the effects of all our actions will be made clear to us. Armies of virtuous AIs, and an almost too perfectly despicable enemy, will rectify all our mistakes with mild punishment or a defeat so clear anyone will be able to recognize it. Even the most cynical person and the biggest anarchist can believe in the rightness of their rulers, the way we can today. My father says there's been nothing like it in history."

"So that's why you think about what will come afterward. Even if circumstances or ideologies change, you want something everyone can value, right?" said Orville.

"Yes, I keep saying I'm hoping that day will come."

"But actually, that's what you're afraid of."

"Afraid? I don't think so. No, I'm sure I'm not."

Orville casually rolled on top of her. His chest pressed into delightful softness. He stroked her hair—now undone, finally. "Humanity has been fighting and winning ever since you were born. Winning the war means any victories after that will pale in comparison. There might be civil strife, there might be secession. Doesn't that scare you?"

"Sure, I suppose that could happen. If there's no enemy, creating one is something we humans do. But that doesn't scare me," she answered.

"You're one tough lady."

"What? No, just the opposite. What I mean is, next to losing you, nothing could scare me." Sayaka cradled Orville's face in her hands and looked into his eyes. She chuckled dryly, then expression left her face. "We could always run away."

"Not a good idea," Orville said, and he kissed her deeply. Then he whispered in her ear, "I can't lie to you. I don't want to run away. The human species needs Messengers to fight for them. I have no doubts about that. I couldn't throw that away and choose you, even if the people who made me allowed it. I'm at peace with my mission."

"So much for seduction."

"Damn it, can't you understand?"

He embraced her powerfully and she responded. When words failed them, they communed with their bodies. But no matter how much this taught the lovers about each other, it left them both resigned to the impossibility of knowing everything.

Their four months together were over all too soon. As

Orville's deployment crept closer, they quarreled occasionally, but never enough to drive them apart. Once, however, Sayaka suggested they take a shuttle to tour one of the huge, near-lightspeed vessels docked in space. Orville sensed what was on her mind but said nothing till she'd circled the giant ship once, then veered away. After insertion into the return trajectory to Triton, Orville finally spoke.

"Thanks."

"For what?"

"For turning back. You were thinking about stowing away, weren't you? Once you'd boarded one of those ships, you would never come back. Not in this lifetime. But I'm glad you didn't."

"You really think so?" said Sayaka.

"Yes, because every one of those ships orbiting the Sun is restricted to port until we Messengers are deployed. They don't want us running away. There's no way we could have gone."

"They think of everything." She exhaled as if surprised and shook her head. "But that's not what I meant. I was asking whether you really thought I wanted to run."

"Don't you?" said Orville.

"No." She shook her head. Orville knew she wasn't telling the truth, but he didn't want to deny her decision to lie. "We're counting on you, Orville."

We, as in humanity.

Two-tenths of the Messengers slated for deployment—nearly fifty thousand—were on Triton. There were many couples like Orville and Sayaka, and as the day approached, the change in the city's mood was apparent. Each couple had felt as if the world were theirs alone. Now they all knew that was impossible.

On the day of deployment, Orville spotted Sayaka from the gangway leading to his ship. She was part of a crowd—

an astonishingly large crowd—united in the sorrow of parting. Orville called to Alexandr boarding ahead of him. "Shumina is here."

"I know." His massive bulk disappeared into the ship without looking back.

Orville turned. His keen vision picked out Sayaka looking toward him bravely, without tears. *Of course*, he thought. They had said their farewells quite exhaustively the previous night. Orville would hardly have minded if she hadn't come today.

But she did come. She had something more to say to him. She opened her mouth wide and slowly formed the words.

"See you. Again. Someday."

The instant Orville saw that, he felt a stabbing pain in his chest. He fled into the ship.

• ◆ •

A Lagrangian point, between the orbits of Jupiter and Saturn. Hundreds of spacecraft were assembling here, where the gravitational pull from the giant planets was in stable equilibrium. The time fleet was coming together.

"Several years ago, the ETs deployed a portion of their total energy to execute a time jump. Based on measurements of the radiant energy liberated in this maneuver, we estimate they reached a point roughly 480 years in the past. There appears to be no purpose to this move other than to change the course of history. We believe they have realized their disadvantage and are moving to eradicate humanity at a point in the past where we were far weaker than we are today."

Orville was not well versed in the technology of temporal upstreaming or the theory of spacetime on which it was based—the technology had been perfected by human scientists working with specialized AIs—but as a Messenger, he understood and could pilot the hardware that made the theory's predictions manifest reality. Orville was not particularly interested in the underlying ideas. If the ETs fled backward in time, he knew how to follow them. That was enough.

"You will now upstream into the past and defeat the enemy, supported by all the matériel and AIs that Sol System has been able to assemble. The situation on the ground, and the enemy's strength, are completely unknown. You may well find your forces inadequate. Therefore, your prime objective isn't to engage the enemy directly, but to alert the local population to the danger and assist them in developing their fighting capabilities to the highest possible level. You will inform and guide, so humanity can fight to defend itself and its future."

But that future was not this present. Orville's face twisted with the pain of that knowledge. Spurring humanity to fight the ET in the past would change history, generating new timestreams. Even if Orville survived the fighting, entered cryostasis and waited long enough, he would not be able to return to *this* present. Regardless of the war's outcome, a completely transformed Sol System would await the Messengers.

He would never see Sayaka again. But if that were all he had to bear—as if that weren't enough—he could have borne it.

"Please access AI Prime and authenticate." At these words from the human officer assigned to see them off, the Messengers closed their eyes and contacted the fleet command AI through their internal comm links. They verified their mission and its implications: they were soldiers who would never return. Using the comm link had been an occasional necessity on Triton, where someone might have been listening, but at this point it was an empty ceremony.

"Authentication is complete. I will now reveal a piece of highly classified information. Our scientists and AIs have just concluded with a high degree of certainty that humanity in this timestream will soon be extinct." The officer choked with emotion. As the one designated to deliver this message, he would have been chosen for his steady nerves, but his voice was trembling.

"The basis for this conclusion is the fact that no Messengers have arrived from our future. If we had been successful against the ET, mankind should also have sent additional Messengers from our own future to help deal with the conflicts we now face. Techniques to determine the timing of arrival of these new hypothetical Messengers have advanced significantly. But as of today, no new Messengers have upstreamed to our present. This means that the ability to deploy new Messengers into the past is not a part of our future. That means we have no future.

"We will be extinct before long, either through defeat or self-destruction. It does not matter." In point of fact, for Orville and the other Messengers about to depart into the past, this was not critically important. Their efforts would spawn new timestreams, in one of which humanity might survive, and that was all that mattered. *If only those four months had never been...*

Sayaka, her friends, and all Triton would vanish in fire. Orville had known this was likely since his inception, but he had pushed it to the back of his mind; conditions might have changed for the better during the past four months. But in the end, the miracle was not to be. Now there was nothing for the Messengers to do but leave these people to their fate.

Orville clenched his fists. *Sayaka,* he cried out inwardly. *Forgive me.* He couldn't save her, but he could take her hopes with him, graven on his heart. *Devotion to humanity.*

"Therefore, we who are about to die entrust our hopes to all humanity across the multiverse, and command you: Carry the word. Triumph. Farewell." The officer disembarked.

The command AI spoke:

"Good morning, Messengers. I am Cutty Sark, Mission AI. I will accompany you to the ends of time, coordinate Upstreamer Force operations and provide support through a wide range of resources. Please initiate sensory suspension. This fleet will now upstream into the past."

The fleet's ships, fortresses, and mobile bases powered down and engaged their chronoshift devices. In the darkness, Orville clamped his teeth and suppressed a scream. *What am I supposed to save?*

Then consciousness winked out. The fleet dropped into the well of time.

Chapter 3

The sound of the great gong, a reverberation in the pit of the stomach, penetrated to the innermost rooms of the palace. A continuous drizzle fell from the low-hanging clouds that almost seemed to graze the palace roofline. The heat was suffocating. The entrance to the thatched Great Hall stood open, but the stench of the attendants arrayed on either side of Miyo fouled the breathless air. She sat waiting, back straight, drenched in sweat.

A man from the future.

A great conflict between men and mononoké in a world yet to be. A voyage to the past to end the war before it begins. Such was not difficult for Miyo to comprehend, at least the idea of it was not; she too often wished to go back in time and do things differently. But she had no notion of how such a journey might be accomplished. That night in Kan's village, she learned how the soldier was given life in the future and how he was sent by the ruler of that world as a harbinger of danger. While the Messenger had not spoken of it, Miyo sensed he had left something behind in that world. Perhaps for him this was a journey with no return. Miyo recalled that moment on Mount Shiki when she was ready to abandon everything, and thought perhaps she understood something of what he felt.

And yet the weariness emanating from this man's core seemed to come from something else. Miyo did not know how long ago he left his country, but he did not seem the sort to be tormented by homesickness. Was this not something deeper—some burden of sorrow he could not lay down? Miyo had not been able to ask him. That night in Kan's village, they stayed up till dawn, hurriedly making plans, agreeing to restage their meeting for the ministers. The Messenger yielded to Miyo's insistence on receiving him as Queen Himiko, with all the proper ceremony. He even made a proposal to render the performance more effective.

"To make a fuss about my being the Messenger of the Laws won't guarantee cooperation from your ministers. We need to engage their self-interest."

"Well, I suppose you're right," answered Miyo. "So?"

"So we're going to give them a little motivation to accept me," said Orville.

"How?"

"It so happens that the perfect event is about to take place. Cutty? How does it look?"

"You are correct. Our Wasps indicate the timing is perfect." The speaking sword and the Messenger began conferring at length. That of course was strange enough, but the Messenger seemed so used to this sort of manipulation that Miyo felt a twinge of concern. Subterfuge seemed to come so naturally to him.

It took ten days to lay the groundwork. On the pretext of querying the gods concerning the state of the kingdom, Miyo deliberately performed a singular divination. Then she ordered that preparations be made in accordance with the oracle; that morning, a detachment of soldiers set out to find the Messenger. Here at the palace, the vigil would continue until their return.

The distant murmur of peasant voices fell silent, replaced by the approaching tread of massed marchers. The elite detachment of three hundred had returned. They crossed the moat surrounding the palace, entered the stockade, marched past the line of small huts belonging to the ministers, and reached the forecourt of the Great Hall. Miyo could hear the neighing of their mounts and the shouts of soldiers warning onlookers—*stand back!*

Kan entered through the sunlit doorway. He stopped three paces before Miyo and prostrated himself. "They have returned. Lord Mimaso performs the ceremony of greeting."

"Where is Takahikoné?"

"Lord Ikima leads the palanquin guard. To protect the Messenger from disturbance by the masses, so he says." Miyo felt a stab of apprehension. *Takahikoné, are you up to something reckless?* As Lord Ikima of Yamatai, Takahikoné retained sole power over administrative affairs of state. This gave him greater influence than Mimaso, who was responsible for religious ritual, or Mimakaki, the chiefdom's master of ritual protocol. Indeed, Takahikoné was effectively the ruler of Yamatai. As shaman Queen Himiko, Miyo ostensibly ranked above him, and Takahikoné humbled himself before her as her "younger brother," but this was merely a pretense to ensure the fealty of other chiefdoms. Beyond that, Takahikoné would never allow Miyo to overshadow him.

He would surely be harboring suspicions toward this strange visitor Miyo had summoned, however exalted that visitor might be. Might Takahikoné be seeking an opportunity to assassinate the Messenger? *No, that was unlikely,* Miyo thought with a shake of her head. It was too early. He would wait, see how events developed. After all, his visitor was creator of the Laws. Perhaps he could be turned to good use, like Miyo had been, to help Takahikoné govern. And if he became a hindrance, disposing of one man would be a simple matter when the time was right. Now was not the time to show his hand.

Yes, that was what Takahikoné would be thinking. He was cold-blooded, but also an adroit tactician. Still, these were all assumptions; he likely assumed that Miyo would continue to behave as he expected. If she did something out of character, how would he respond?

From the forecourt came the sound of Mimaso's shrill peroration. Second after Takahikoné in the hierarchy of Yamatai, this timid, gaunt man was in fact Lord Ikima's errand boy. His nervousness was audible in the hoarse quavering of his unimpressive, birdlike voice. As she listened, Miyo rose serenely to her feet.

"My lady...?" Miyo's maidservants turned toward her with doubting eyes. When Miyo stepped forward they raised an outcry. "It is forbidden! You cannot leave. You will be defiled!"

Miyo called out for Kan. As arranged, the boy quickly took his place behind Miyo. The women tried to follow; he brandished his sword. Miyo cast a glance at her terrified maidservants and swiftly strode outside. Under lowering skies, the scene in the forecourt spread out before her.

The Messenger sat cross-legged on a palanquin, surrounded by three hundred or more soldiers drawn up in ranks. His regal bearing was visible even at this distance. Before him were Mimaso and the ministers of state. They knelt respectfully in the mud, but Miyo guessed they were inwardly annoyed. They would fail to appreciate the significance of this ceremony for the Messenger of the Laws. An envoy from Great Wei might deserve such protocol. But this man?

The peasants permitted to watch the ceremony lined the opposite sides of the forecourt, with guards standing at intervals in front of them. Commoners were not usually allowed in the palace, but Miyo's oracle required their presence. They seemed not so much bored with the proceedings as eager to return to the fields. Summer was no time to be away from their crops.

Then the peasants began to understand what was happening. A buzz of curious voices gradually turned to cries of amazement as Miyo resolutely gazed down on them, her face an expressionless mask.

"Who is that?"

"A lady in waiting?"

"You fool! It's Queen Himiko!"

Standing on her dais beneath the eaves of the Great Hall, Miyo was arrayed for a divination: white hempen tunic, hem dyed madder red, her bronze mirror glittering on her breast. She was bedecked with necklaces of pearls and *magatama*, curved beads of quartz and jade. She held a bronze wand in one hand and a long staff adorned with star anise leaves in the other. Her blue-black mottled tattoo ran from cheek to breast, and her entire body was decorated with rope patterns in ground cinnabar. Her maidservants had tried to dissuade her, warning that the patterns would run in the heat, but Miyo insisted. Tattoos were quite common in this land, yet she knew—she had carefully calculated— that her appearance would be met with awe by her subjects. This was their first glimpse of their queen, and her raiment had to be conspicuous enough to spark immediate recognition.

The peasants dropped to their knees like a stand of grass flattened by the wind. As she glared at the throng, Miyo smiled inwardly at the effect she'd created.

Just then Mimaso's long speech finally drew to a close.

The Great Hall was behind him, and he remained oblivious to Miyo. Following the usual protocol, the yeomen holding the palanquin now lowered it to the ground, like dolls moving in unison. Mimaso stepped forward to escort the Messenger to the ministers' quarters.

"Messenger of the Laws!"

Miyo's shout rang through the forecourt. Mimaso spun round, incredulous. "Queen Himiko?"

Miyo descended the rough-hewn steps. Without a glance at Mimaso, she strode toward the palanquin, splashing muddy water. She planted her staff, fell to her knees and prostrated herself deeply before him.

"Himiko of Yamatai welcomes you. Pray come with me."

The Messenger stepped down from the litter, nodded, and stood next to Miyo. When she looked up, his hand was stretched toward her. Miyo couldn't help but frown. True, she had not warned him against any show of familiarity. When they were making plans, he had asked her if there were any taboos to be avoided. She'd told him not to be concerned about details of protocol, to simply maintain a calm and regal bearing. What a blunder. Still, it would not do for her to spurn his outstretched hand, so Miyo took it respectfully, without the least eye contact, and turned toward the Great Hall. Now all that remained was to get him inside.

It was then that she noticed the other man—his long, looped braids, the imposing beard, the rugged visage. He was standing next to Mimaso, who stood stiffly at attention as if he'd swallowed a pole.

It was Takahikoné.

He must have come, still wearing his sword, straight through the ranks of soldiers arrayed across the forecourt. His face twitched with irritation, as if he might start bellowing at any moment. But that would hardly be necessary. His opinion of Miyo's brazen breach of protocol was written in his face. Miyo had to seize the initiative.

"Your manners, Lord Ikima!" she called out. "Before you stands the Messenger of the Laws, bringer of the rules of Heaven and Earth!"

Mimaso threw himself to the ground with almost comical zeal. Takahikoné merely dipped his head and strode brusquely toward Miyo. The Messenger whispered, "I'll speak to him."

"No! The common people cannot hear the voice of the god," said Miyo. Naturally, otherwise her authority would evaporate.

Takahikoné strode up, dropped to his knees in the mud alongside Miyo and called out in a commanding voice, for all to hear. "I am Lord Ikima, Takahikoné of Yamatai. You will forgive my insolence in addressing one so intimate with Himiko our queen. But as she is our queen, I beg you not to place her alongside you, but to return her to us."

Miyo suppressed a scowl. She might have expected this. If Takahikoné's aim was to reproach her indirectly, she could repay him in his own coin here and now, using the pretense of speaking for the Messenger. But Takahikoné had ignored her and addressed the Messenger directly. This required a direct reply. His gambit was in itself an act of insolence toward Miyo, but with his words he had paid her homage. His greeting could not be ignored.

"Ikima..." Miyo groped for words, anything to create a delay, but the Messenger stopped her. As she turned to him, he winked. With a flourish, he drew the sword from over his shoulder and presented it to her.

The instant Miyo grasped the hilt of the heavy blade, it shone with a glare like the risen sun. A mighty voice, neither male nor female, began to declaim in ringing tones.

"Know this, Himiko Queen of Yamatai! Guard against

discord, strive for unity, turn aside antagonism and mistrust. For your realm stands in peril!"

Takahikoné's jaw sagged with astonishment. If this man with mettle second to none was affected thus, it was no surprise that the rest of the host were unable even to raise their eyes from the mud. Miyo too was awestruck, but not too much to notice the Messenger's dry smile, hidden from the others by the sword's brilliance.

Even before the light faded, a commotion rose from the direction of the palace gate. They could hear a horse neighing as it was reined to a halt. A lone soldier rushed into the forecourt and stopped, struck dumb by the scene before him. Miyo quickly spied him among the rest, called to one of Takahikoné's captains and sent him to question the man. The captain returned, looking thunderstruck, and began conferring with Takahikoné.

"At the Tsuge border crossing? Kukochihiko, that scoundrel!" Takahikoné's face was dark with rage.

"There was an attack," said Miyo. Takahikoné started at the sound of Miyo's voice, turned about, then instantly assumed a calm visage. He nodded.

"Mounted soldiers and peasant footmen from the east, from Kunu. They press over our borders, spreading chaos."

"This is why the Messenger favors us with his presence." Just then the light from the sword faded out. Miyo's words were heard by everyone present. They looked up with open astonishment. Miyo had known this was coming, but she could only marvel at the sword's ability to guess the timing of the soldiers' arrival to the day and minute.

Takahikoné's eyes narrowed, as if he suspected some trickery. Miyo checked her urge to smile. She had the upper hand. There was nothing to be gained by pressing the point.

"Prepare for battle, then." Miyo took the Messenger by the hand into the Great Hall. As if a spell had been lifted, the host began to stir. Takahikoné's bellowing for his captains rose above the tumult of voices.

• ◆ •

To Miyo's surprise, it was Takahikoné himself who proposed that the Messenger be at the head of the troops, and furthermore, that Miyo should attend and assist him. She wondered if he had already accepted the Messenger's authority, but things did not smell quite right.

"Lord Ikima has appointed Takahaya, Hayato of Kumaso, to lead the army. The captains are all his compatriots." Kan brought news overheard from the ministers. These Hayato warriors from Kumaso had sworn an oath to Yamatai; their prowess and loyalty had earned them a place in Takahikoné's bodyguard. Appointing Takahaya to lead the troops meant Lord Ikima had no thought of giving real authority to the Messenger, much less Miyo. With both of them away from the palace, Takahikoné would have a free hand, as the Messenger himself pointed out.

Nonetheless, Miyo accepted his proposal. Five days later, a force of five thousand warriors assembled. After rituals to ensure their success, they set off. Miyo and the Messenger rode in separate palanquins. Iga, their destination, lay 250 *ri* northeast of Makimuku. The march would take three days.

Sure enough, Miyo's palanquin was in the middle of the column while the Messenger's litter was at the head. They were not allowed to be together despite Takahikoné's suggestion that she assist him. Not only that, no runner was permitted to come and go between their palanquins. But the Messenger had given Miyo a *magatama* bead that allowed her to communicate with him over the two *ri* of the column separating them.

"What do you think Takahikoné is up to?" said the Messenger.

"When the ruler is absent, the minister who is left behind dreams of taking the throne. Such has been the way of the world since the beginning. But Takahikoné would not do that. Not yet. It would hardly please the other chieftains. While he strengthens his position, he probably hopes we will meet with some unexpected accident."

"That sounds rather unpleasant."

Miyo stirred restlessly inside the tiny palanquin draped with a wickerwork screen to shield her from prying eyes. A merry, masculine laugh sounded from the *magatama*. "Never fear. Kan will protect us. That boy shows promise."

Kan was strolling along behind the slaves carrying Miyo's litter, a fearsome short sword—bestowed on him by the Messenger—tucked into the folds of his tunic. Miyo, her spirits raised, spoke into the bead. "Keep your wits about you. Those Hayato from Kumaso are deft enough to pluck out your very liver without you being the wiser."

"No one's getting my liver," answered the Messenger coolly. "Tell me about the enemy. As far as I know, this clash with Kunu was supposed to take place sometime later. Are there frequent battles between Yamatai and Kunu?"

"Of course not. And since I became queen, not once. Kunu knows its place. I must confess I have no idea why they attack us now. I always thought Kukochihiko was a reasonable man. Messenger O, don't you know why this is happening?"

"We don't know the motivation. But a large mass of people, some bearing arms, are pressing toward Iga from the east." This was the sword speaking. Miyo was slowly becoming accustomed to the Messenger's miracles; now she felt the urge to learn something basic.

"A question, sword."

"Cutty, if you please," answered the sword.

"Where are you, Cutty?"

"Where am I? I am everywhere."

"Don't be sly. You cast your voice from a distance with the same magic as this bead, do you not?" said Miyo.

"Very good," replied the sword. Miyo heard the Messenger choking back a laugh. The sword was silent a moment, then: "Yes. My body is in a certain location. From there, I control eyes and ears all over the world. But don't tell anyone. This is important strategic information."

"Are you the Messenger's wife?" asked Miyo.

"Excuse me?" Again the Messenger's laughter spilled from the *magatama*. The sword's voice was disapproving. "The answer is no. The Messenger does not marry. No, you do not understand the feelings of AIs like us. Romance arises when there is something about an individual that another cannot understand."

"You needn't become so upset about it," said Miyo.

"I am not upset!"

"Queen Himiko! Miyo!" The Messenger sounded as if he'd laugh himself sick. "No human has ever cornered Cutty like that," he said finally.

The sword cut in, "This is no time for idle chatter."

"I know. I hear it too. We've got a lot of Wasps deployed," said the Messenger.

"Coverage over the entire Ueno basin," said Cutty. "I confirm multiple sonic signatures of bronze-edged weapons cutting timber and human flesh—the sounds of battle. I'm detecting elevated temperatures and hydrocarbon particles. There are fires."

"Looks like we're ready to put on a demonstration," said the Messenger.

"You will join the battle?" asked Miyo.

"The only thing that light show is going to earn me is a little respect, nothing more. I have to follow it up with a feat of arms." They had discussed this already before setting out. Miyo realized that her concern for the Messenger's safety was personal. She dropped any pretense that it was otherwise. "Be careful. The Emishi are deadly bowmen," she warned.

"Save your worries for the enemy," answered the Messenger. "Sometimes I don't know when to stop killing."

"Don't be a fool," Miyo murmured, as the dull baying of bamboo war trumpets began sounding along the column, a wave of activity spreading down the ranks. The trumpets sounded again and again, captains marshalling their men. There was a clatter of drawn swords and the pounding of running feet. Men with whips moved horses and oxen in the baggage train off to the side of the path. Miyo lifted the edge of the screen and peered out.

They were in a ravine, with open country a short distance ahead. The narrow way ran along a small stream. Even with no head for tactics, Miyo could see the danger of an ambush here. But Takahaya was already reinforcing his vanguard and sending small parties of soldiers running up the sides of the ravine and along the stream to flush out any enemies lying in wait.

Miyo heard a noise behind her and turned to see Kan's narrow face peering into the palanquin. "Lady Miyo, we are moving you to the rear. It is dangerous here."

"No. I will stay." Then she realized Kan did not know of the Messenger's plans, and added: "The Messenger will join the battle. There's nothing to fear."

"But my lady..." Kan seemed to be groping for words— *No matter how strong he is, how much difference can he make?* Miyo tried another tack.

"Go forward and see what's happening, then come back and tell me. I can't go myself."

"I won't leave your side," said Kan.

"It's all right. Hear that? The trumpets are sounding the advance. I'll be safe here. And you want to prove yourself, don't you?"

"But..." Still Kan hesitated, so Miyo pointed through the gap in the screen. "Look, they've raised the banners!"

Near the front ranks, a huge yellow banner, double the span of a man's arms, soared above the host. Never before had this awe-inspiring war flag, trimmed in threads of gold, been raised in battle. Years before, it had been sent to Wa as a gift from the great empire of Wei. The banner's four Chinese characters—*Ruler of Wa, Friend of Wei*—rustled in the breeze, a proclamation to all from the emperor across the sea.

A great battle cry rose from the host. Miyo smiled as she saw Kan's eyes widen with childlike wonder. He ran excitedly toward the vanguard.

At last the sounds of battle came from the direction of the front, but died down almost immediately. This was not part of the plan. Apparently this was not a full-scale engagement. Miyo spoke to the *magatama*. "Messenger O? What is happening?"

"Apparently just a detachment of enemy pathfinders. We're starting the search for the main body. You there, give me that horse!" The Messenger took someone's mount. Miyo said no more, not wanting to distract him. The war trumpets sounded again, and the column lurched into motion.

They left the ravine and moved into open country. Here and there across the plain, which was half the expanse of Yamatai, Miyo could see smoke rising from dwellings that had been set ablaze. Still, something was wrong—war banners and the glitter of helmet and armor were nowhere to be seen. Where were the enemy forces?

Miyo was restless with anxiety but the *magatama* was

silent, even as the column entered one of the villages. The order to stand was handed down to bivouac, and Miyo took her midday meal in a large house in the village. Not till the sun began its journey down the sky did the bead speak again. But the tone of that voice made Miyo uneasy.

"Miyo."

"What happened? Are you safe?" she asked.

"I'm returning now," said the Messenger. "I was delayed."

"What do you mean? Are you hurt? Tell me!" But there was no answer.

Finally Kan returned, his face flushed with the excitement of combat. "Lady Miyo, victory is ours. I dispatched one of them myself. He was attacking a farmer; we crossed blades—"

"I was worried about you. I waited long," said Miyo.

"I'm sorry." Abashed and reminded of his responsibilities to Miyo, Kan dipped his head in respect.

Miyo smiled; she was relieved to see him unharmed. "Did you see the Messenger fight the enemy?" she asked.

"I saw him. He fought from horseback, wielding his long sword. He scattered the Emishi like dolls. No arrow found him, no spear made him flinch. He is terribly strong. All the men were in awe of him."

"He is unhurt, then?" asked Miyo.

"Not even a scratch."

Then why had he seemed so downhearted just now? As she mulled this over, a voice called from outside. Kan went to see. When he returned he was frowning.

"Takahaya blathers about an audience. A man of his station! You needn't pay any attention, I think."

"Wait," said Miyo. "What does he want?"

"He said an envoy from the enemy wants to speak with you directly. Why don't they just drive the envoy away?"

"An Emishi messenger?" said Miyo. This was peculiar;

a war declaration or a request for parley could simply be passed to Takahaya, Lord Ikima's proxy. To request an audience with Himiko herself suggested something extraordinary. Miyo motioned Kan away and whispered into the *magatama*. "Messenger O! One of the Emishi requests an audience. I believe I should speak with him. What say you?"

"Yes, go ahead—no, I'll meet him too. Come, I'm in Takahaya's quarters."

Shielded from the eyes of the common folk by an entourage of twenty maidservants in place of the usual screens, Miyo arrived at Takahaya's pavilion. She hadn't long to wait before the coarse-faced Hayato commander arrived to prostrate himself before her with an air of extreme discomfiture. Inside, the Messenger sat cross-legged on an improvised dais, waiting. Miyo sat beside him.

Takahaya's country was far to the west. With no inkling of protocol in the palace at Yamatai and no conception concerning the proper way to host these two luminaries, he barked for someone to bring sake and sweets, and set them timidly before his two guests. He was so subservient it seemed pointless to talk to him.

"Why is he so ill at ease? Did something happen?" Miyo whispered to Kan.

"The Messenger caught a stray arrow with his bare hands before it struck him."

So that was it. Takahaya must have been astounded. But knowing that actually made her task easier. Miyo shifted to face Kan directly. "The Messenger is pleased with this hospitality. Our host will do well to persevere."

"Takahaya, the Queen speaks thus—" Kan began, parroting Miyo. Evidently heartened, Takahaya recovered his good spirits and offered words of thanks. Miyo began to feel favorably disposed toward this simple soldier. "It is said that a messenger from the Emishi is nearby. May he be brought here?" she asked. Kan repeated, Takahaya answered.

"Begging your pardon, but he said he would gut himself unless he saw the Queen, and we cannot send him away. We threatened to behead him, but he offered his neck and told us to do as we pleased. His spirit would return to settle the score."

"Fear not, just bring him to me." Miyo paused; she might have sounded a trifle insouciant. "Bind his eyes and limbs, that he may cause no trouble," she added.

Soon the man was brought in, bound hand and foot and slung from a pole, like a boar ready for roasting.

"I am Himiko, Queen of Yamatai. What have you to say, Emishi?" As she spoke, Miyo noticed that the Messenger seemed depressed.

Even hanging from his pole, the Emishi's reply was firm and resolute. "So you are the queen? Then hear the words of my king, who speaks thus: our realm is invaded by an army of mononoké. All is chaos. We beg you, oh queen, grant grain and meat to our families and kinsmen. Help us. If you do, we swear we will quell the mononoké and destroy them."

"What?" Miyo was so astonished, she forgot to speak through Kan. "Mononoké—attacking Kunu?"

"They destroy the mountains, they destroy the rivers. They are *here*." The Emishi spoke with the fearless resignation of one without a homeland to return to.

"Then those who overran the barrier were not attacking. They were fleeing," said Miyo.

"Yes. We beg your forgiveness."

The Messenger turned wordlessly to Miyo. She knew the reason for the despair in his eyes. She dismissed everyone so they could be alone.

"Do you not know where the mononoké are?" she asked.

"I will. There's a surveillance network already being put into place. But I didn't expect they'd time their arrival with such accuracy. I thought we'd have up to twenty years before they got here. I let down my guard."

"All Wasps deployed for airborne mining surveys are redirected to Kunu. The surveillance net should be in place within eight hours." This was the sword.

"It's too late," said the Messenger. "We have to abandon this area. Miyo, get ready to retreat before dawn. We have to establish a defensive line with fortifications in that ravine we passed through today. The refugees we can gather by morning should be sent to Yamatai. The rest will have to fend for themselves. And runners must be sent to the capital. Every available soldier should be called up."

"Is it…is it really that urgent?" said Miyo.

"The first refugees came more than ten days ago. I don't know how many fighters Kunu has left. But against the ET, at the breakout stage in their life cycle? They're probably already dead."

Miyo gasped. The Messenger looked away and whispered bitterly. "This isn't the first time I've blundered."

"Not the first time?"

"I arrived before them, but I didn't prepare soon enough. I was routed."

Defeat was the shadow hanging over this man. Remorse for everyone he had failed to save during his years of struggle. Before Miyo had a chance to respond, the Messenger took his helmet and stood up.

"I have to check the front line. I leave the rest to you. Cutty, we have a critical. Send backup, and from the other side of the planet if you have to."

"Confirm—no, stand by. I'm getting criticals from other stations now."

The Messenger stared at the sword. It spoke again. "The

Kingdom of Aksum in East Africa: a Messenger in cryostasis has been attacked and destroyed. Consequently Giza Station is no more. Friendly forces are being urgently wakened from cryostasis on Mounts Athos and Tahat, in Qal'at Jarmo and all Middle Eastern stations. Nearby stations are earmarked for backup."

"Damn it!"

The Messenger kicked violently at a nearby crate and stomped off.

Chapter 4

When they arrived in the Sol System of the early twenty-second century, the Messengers first carried out surveys to confirm that none of the signature strongholds and structures associated with ET replication were extant. Earth was still wrapped in tranquility, its blue surface adorned with masses of white clouds.

Having stolen a march on the enemy, the Messengers celebrated, then hurried toward Earth to warn of the coming crisis. On the way, they detected signs of human activity on Mars. Settlements were under construction, using materials from Earth and the Moon. Large groups of robots were at work on the surface, clustered at the poles and around subsurface water sources. An encouraging sight, and expected from history as the Messengers knew it. Humans in this era were moving out into the cosmos, even if their capabilities were still undeveloped. The Messengers assumed that cooperation in engaging the enemy would be forthcoming.

Making contact with the people of the twenty-second century and convincing them that the Messengers came from the future went easily enough. The peoples of Earth took one look at the space fleet of several hundred units, carrying Messengers fluent in all of Earth's languages, and welcomed them as brothers. The politicians were wary and the scientists more than skeptical, but once they received background information on the Messengers' deployment—with explanations concerning the theory and practice of temporal upstreaming—they agreed to cooperate.

Yet everything from that point on had been fraught with difficulty. There was no Earth organization in the twenty-second century with the capacity to set a course for humanity. The United Nations was potentially the nucleus of such an endeavor, but it remained weaker than its sovereign members. The governments of Earth had grave reservations about taking collective action—military action—at the suggestion of an entirely unknown entity against yet another unknown entity. Still, this sort of resistance had been anticipated, which is why the Messengers were dispatched to the past in human form.

What helped the Messengers was the discovery of several enemy colonies already on Earth. One was found in the European city of Köln, another in the Chinese coal center of Fushun. The intruders were probably a vanguard of reconnaissance rather than a full-scale invasion. Eradicating these colonies required most of the military resources of the respective states, and the threat of mass invasion caused the General Assembly to pass their resolution. Finally, the governments of Earth understood that the ET represented a new and unknown challenge, along with the epidemics, famines, ethnic conflicts, and environmental devastation that continued to bedevil humanity. But even then, some leaders suggested that the Messengers themselves might be responsible for the two colonies, planting them in order to profit from the resulting conflict.

Regardless, a structure for cooperation was established to meet the threat. In accordance with the UN resolution,

Earth began strengthening its air defense and surface combat capabilities. The Messengers were responsible for space-based defense. At least that was the plan.

• ◆ •

Preparations for resisting the ET advanced at a snail's pace. Five months after the arrival of the Messengers, modifications to the targeting programs for near-Earth orbit nuclear strike missiles—which Earth already had in quantity—were complete. All of Earth's observatories were integrated into the space defense net or soon would be. But that was roughly all that had been accomplished. Production of anti-ET weapon systems had not yet started. Earth's off-world production plants were reluctant to repurpose, and not a single factory was focusing its efforts on preparation for battle. Lunar mining operations, robot factories, launch platforms, solar power installations—everywhere the Messengers turned, they met with foot-dragging and resistance. The red tape even extended to construction of the Messengers' own facilities.

Even the slow pace of manufacturing arrangements was tolerable compared to the progress of talks dealing with control of UN Forces. Here things had completely bogged down. The Messengers were whipsawed between the great powers that had long dominated the planet and the smaller nations that had been increasing their leverage since the turn of the millennium. It was impossible to predict when the chain of command for UN Forces would be decided upon.

Cutty was in despair. Even her most urgent task, a planet-wide screening for ET spores, was blocked at the outset. She was only authorized to conduct fragmentary searches, country by country, as each individually gave—and then sometimes withdrew—permission. Earth never seemed to understand that even one missed spore could replicate into a huge horde. Nevertheless, Cutty was completely overloaded. Along with her screening work, she dispatched a fleet of more than a hundred vessels to Venus on a major search and destroy mission.

In the twenty-sixth century, the enemy had used Venus as a seed bed. Now, Cutty carried out a thorough search for underground bases or colonies hidden beneath the thick atmosphere that shrouded this world. Sure enough, several large colonies were discovered. One after another they were wiped out with thermonuclear warheads—for the Messengers were no more than weapons of medium power. After the strikes, thorough mop-up operations were carried out to ensure that not a single spore had escaped.

The forces allocated to the Messengers amounted to everything that humanity in the twenty-sixth century could assemble, but those forces were still hard-pressed to cover two planets as well as the countless small bodies orbiting the Sun. Their main energy source was antimatter brought from the future, but supplies were not inexhaustible. A long-term conflict would mean building antimatter production plants. The twenty-second century lacked the facilities necessary to support the operations of the fleet, which forced the Messengers to rely on local help. To give up on humanity—that is, to conduct operations without them—was not a realistic option.

"We blew the Hamersley Range mining deal?" Orville was on a break. As part of the Messengers' call for assistance from Earth, they had even gotten involved in deal-making, offering technology in exchange for access to resources. Orville's colleague in Sydney replied:

"The cabinet members were rolling their eyes during the entire meeting. I explained that if we leveled the mountains, they'd be able to access several times as much ore as they do now, but they couldn't stomach the loss of wildlife habitat and tribal homelands. The whole group walked out in a huff before I was even finished. What's more important to them, the history of their country or the future of humanity?"

"History's just an idea. The urge to sacrifice yourself for it isn't something they can develop overnight," said Orville. Then he paused; his own use of the word "history" troubled him. The word usually refers to the past. Did it make sense to use *history* to refer to things that have not yet occurred? The future seemed weightier than the past.

"Completion rate of negotiations with major corporations is now 45 percent of target." Cutty's expressionless voice cut in. She was capable of communicating with all Messengers simultaneously, but right now she didn't seem to have the processor cycles available to add expressive color to her voice. To Orville she sounded weary.

"The corporations are as bad as their governments. They're completely intractable. The ignorance and delusions of their executives are beyond belief. Even the few corporations with an AI on their management team are obstructing and misrepresenting information. And only 2 percent of corporations have AIs."

"There's not much we can do if they haven't achieved data presence," said Orville. The Messengers' world had full data presence—any public information could be searched from any location, limited only by the speed of light. Except for minor anomalies like Sayaka's Supply Department, it was virtually impossible to suppress, conceal, or be beyond reach of information. If agreement on something was reached in New York, it was taken for granted that Beijing and Mumbai would fall in line within seconds. If a corporation on Mars was found to have cooked its books, its sister companies on Saturn and Uranus would be targets for punishment after a comm lag of only a few hours. Orville was painfully aware of the ignorance and suspicion caused by not having the required information at one's fingertips at all times: endless meetings, deliberations and consultations, inconceivable misunderstanding and hostility.

• ◆ •

A small, high-speed shuttle on the surface of the Moon. The Messengers had been traveling back and forth between Earth's bases, scattered throughout Sol System as far as Mars.

"The launch platform's not available? What's the story?" Orville called on his internal comm circuit.

The voice of the human transport chief at Moon Polar Base North came back in a flat monotone. "Orders from headquarters. If you have a complaint, direct it to them."

"Haven't you heard about the UN resolution? Bases and industrial installations are to render all possible assistance to Century XXVI Upstreamer Forces. I've got to have your cooperation," said Orville.

"We're aware of the resolution, but our government hasn't passed the domestic legislation. We're working to transition our manufacturing processes in time for passage of the new laws. This will require a bit more time."

"We don't have time, the ET could attack at any moment," shouted Orville.

"We're a commercial enterprise. We can't take our facilities offline without compensation."

"You—" Orville cut the comm link and smashed his fist against the wall of the cockpit. "Pig-headed fool!" he muttered.

The four Messengers sitting behind him shrugged or smiled distantly. The voice of Cutty Sark reached their shuttle docked at the terminal adjacent to Polar Base North.

"Still won't budge?" asked Cutty.

"It's no use. Looks like they don't plan to get moving till their butts go up in flames. What about other bases?" said Orville.

"The same everywhere. National governments, big corporations, and private organizations and facilities. I'm meeting resistance at every level. Conflicting ideas, poor communication, key people nowhere to be found or even mentally absent. Demands for kickbacks. Meddling from protestors and skeptics. I've simply no idea how long these delays are going to continue."

"Total gridlock. Unbelievable." The jubilation that had greeted their arrival in this timestream seemed to have evaporated.

"What do we do?" Alexandr asked Orville.

Orville was silent, deep in thought.

"Do we sit tight and wait? These delays aren't going to last forever. If we're going to wait, there's something I'd like to work on," said Alexander.

"What?"

"I'm writing a book."

Orville turned to see that Alexandr was writing by hand in a notebook. "What's all that about?"

"I'm sending it to Triton in a capsule with a beacon. If I drop it off in the vicinity, someone will pick it up in a century or two," said Alexandr.

"Addressed to Shumina?"

"She said I have a talent for words."

"What's your book about?" Orville asked without much interest.

"It's about a bug."

Orville suppressed the urge to roll his eyes at Alexandr's earnest expression. "A bug?" he repeated.

"Yes. A little bug, born on the leaf of a big tree. He has

this nice life, just eating leaves, but one day he notices he's in danger. Something is trying to suck the life out of his tree. So, to avert the danger, he has to travel from his branch to the big tree trunk."

"What's the danger? The ET?" asked Orville.

"Don't say that!" said Alexandr. "If the theme is that obvious, you lose the whole mood. This is children's literature. But who should be the villain? Bees and spiders are so passé." The rough-hewn Messenger was dead serious. Orville watched him write for a while, then stood up.

"If the book's for children, why don't you make the villain a bear? I'm heading out."

"Oh? Going to try negotiating in person?"

"I'm going to put a gun to their heads. Cutty? Hack the base mainframe and cook me up a system status message. Something like 'all systems nominal.' I don't want any company headquarters or governments involved."

"Even if I can fool them at first, they'll notice soon enough," answered Cutty. "If they discover we used force, it will only make things difficult later. I'd very much prefer that you dropped the idea."

"Can't do it. If the ET come down on us it's too late. I need you to print me up a weapon too. A low-powered firearm. No, a sword is better. Projectile weapons are too everyday in this era. Make it as scary-looking as you can."

"Perhaps a uniforge carbon-titanium blade? With electrodischarge semiconductors embedded in the surface to cut, say, stainless steel?"

"I knew you'd like it," said Orville.

The onboard molecular printer was capable of laminar fabrication of anything from food to weapons. The device gave off a faint smell as it whirred into activity. Orville and his team pored over a schematic of the moon base while the sword printed out. Finally, it was ready.

Orville suited up for the walk outside and hefted the sword. It was longer than his arm, with a shimmering, milk-white blade. Alexandr grinned.

"Perfect. The galactic hero. Pure retrofuture."

"Put it in your story," said Orville. "All right. I'll take the lead. The rest of you follow me and do what you need to do." The Messengers left the shuttle and began walking toward the base. The sun on the horizon cast long shadows across the surface.

Orville wondered if he should write something too. A letter? If he sent a capsule now, before a fork in the timestreams, it would travel to all subsequent streams—to those destined to be changed by his journey as well as to those that would remain untouched. Except that he had nothing to say. It would be senseless to write only "I miss you." He envied Alexandr, who had something to share with his beloved. Orville put it out of his mind.

●◆●

The sight of Orville's sword alone was all it took to get instant cooperation from the transport chief, but a single sword could not slice through the oceans of red tape that seemed to straightjacket the Earth. Orville and the other Messengers fumed, frustrated. He thought of the sword and mused on a simpler answer.

"Cutty," said Orville.

"Yes."

"Is there a way to totally eliminate all these delays?"

"Subjugate the planet. You know that." Orville knew. The quickest, simplest solution would be for them to simply notify humanity that they would be taking over all administrative and communication functions. But since this would clearly earn the Messengers a huge amount of hostility, the fact that they had considered it—and had the capability to make that decision a reality—was kept secret.

To hijack Earth, to trample on the fundamental dignity of humanity in this timestream, would be going too far. As it was, the Messengers had already interfered extensively, changing far too much history. At this very moment they were excavating ore deposits that were not supposed to be discovered for another century and altering relationships and genealogies that would otherwise have remained unbroken for two centuries. It was impossible to forecast the impact such actions might have. Their orders were to save humanity, even if it meant rewriting history entirely. But should they do it?

The Messengers decided policy questions via simple majority rule. Any Upstreamer Force AI could call for a referendum on any proposal. With full data presence, the whole process took less than a minute. But Orville never submitted a proposal to take over Earth. Sayaka's convictions about human history somehow weighed heavily on him. During the next three months, other AIs twice called for votes on taking over Earth, but each time the proposal failed to attract even 30 percent support.

The Messengers would regret their decision. But that was later, eleven months after the Messengers' arrival, when the ET onslaught began.

•◆•

The first omen was the firing of multiple lasers from Earth into space.

The lasers' emanations were detected by Earth-based observers and the Messengers' network in space. The initial verdict: in all likelihood a meaningless stunt. The emissions appeared to be aimed at random points in space rather than planets or bases. Only after the attack began did the defenders realize that all the lasers had been aimed at the plane of the ecliptic.

In March of 2210, over a period of twenty hours 14,000 light sources topping 100 million degrees—thermonuclear propulsion signatures—were detected in the asteroid belt. The lights were distributed around the compass. Five hundred more were detected at the same time in the vicinity of Jupiter, shuttling at tremendous velocity between the gas giant and the asteroids. The Messengers immediately issued their highest-level alert and began analyzing the data. It took half a day to reach their conclusion. The ET's strategy was time-consuming yet simple: to overwhelm humanity's defenses and wipe out the planet by simultaneously launching huge numbers of small asteroids on a collision course with Earth. A saturation attack, ancient and brutally straightforward.

The analyst AIs surmised that the ET had arrived in this era before the Messengers and sought concealment, probably to avoid having their customary invasion buildup blocked by the later-arriving Upstream Force; they'd hidden among the moons of Jupiter. Using their propulsion systems only when Jupiter shielded them from Earth, they'd deployed troops and thermonuclear fuel throughout the asteroid belt. While preparing to turn the asteroids into missiles, they had also dispatched a small recon team to Earth's surface. Once the team had completed their target selection, they had fed their data to the asteroid belt by burst transmission and then self-terminated. This had been the cause of the "random" laser firings. As soon as preparations were complete, the asteroids were launched *en masse* toward Earth; once concealment was no longer needed, the ET operated openly from their Jupiter bases to create additional asteroid missiles as fast as possible.

The enemy neutralized the orbital momentum of the asteroids and sent them in free fall toward Earth. The earlier intercept could be achieved, the smaller the warhead needed to divert an asteroid from its trajectory toward Earth, so the Upstreamer Force fired all their thermonuclear and antiproton warheads toward the asteroids and at the moons of Jupiter, overwhelming the 14,000 asteroids heading toward them. Still, there was little chance of total success and no margin for error. Even a single asteroid strike would cause untold damage on Earth.

Humanity's first reaction was to condemn the Messengers for not detecting the threat sooner. Even a child could guess the enemy might use asteroids to strike Earth. The Messengers responded that such a strategy was highly unusual; the ET had never resorted to it during the wars of the twenty-sixth century. In that era, they had taken possession of the Sun and were always completely reliant on large inputs of solar energy. They had never tried something as laborious and inefficient as drawing hydrogen from Jupiter for nuclear fusion. This time as well, the enemy must have actually preferred solar power. This new and different strategy, one that barely met their energy needs, must have been a huge gamble.

Still, there was no denying that the Messengers had blundered. They had brought technology and power from the future—and a high-handed attitude—yet they had been easily outmaneuvered by the enemy. From this point forward, a dark shadow fell over their alliance with Earth.

The fleet's all-out attack was 99.586 percent successful. Fifty-eight asteroids still drifted toward Earth on flattened parabolic trajectories. Though they had exhausted their supplies of antimatter, more nuclear weapons were available. But these were controlled by Earth, and so the balance of power between the allies shifted definitively. Earth's new demands astonished the Messengers: overall command authority, handover of principal fleet elements, transfer of all military and civilian technology. Earth even demanded the right to determine overall policy, now and in the future, out of respect for humanity as ancestors. *We are your progenitors. You exist only because of us. Never forget that debt of gratitude. Defer to our wisdom.*

All this seemed to be, and in fact probably was, the irrational response of a desperate humanity venting its pent-up bitterness. But the Messengers yielded to all of Earth's demands. Their orders were to save humanity by any means possible—even if they had to bear the insults of barbarians from the past. This was no time for petty squabbling.

So, after several weeks spent retrofitting the ships' living quarters to accommodate humans, fleet elements carrying nuclear weapons supplied by Earth conducted attacks under the command of UN Forces officers. These men of Earth acquitted themselves admirably. They may have relied heavily on the Messengers to offset their own rudimentary data-gathering capabilities, but they deployed their warheads accurately and successfully repelled the incoming asteroids. Humanity was defending itself. Their officers were jubilant, and the people of Earth went wild with joy at the news.

Then, in an instant, they plunged from heaven to hell.

They discovered that the ET had inserted cloaked spore colonies through a gap in the off-world surveillance network—a gap created by the difficulties and disputes with humanity. It was assumed that the enemy did not have the ability to interpret the subtleties of human civilization; they probably discovered the gaps in the network based on communication traffic patterns and by movements of the fleet. By the time they were discovered, at least ten colonies had reached maturity on every continent. They began launching attacks on major urban centers and military installations.

Humanity was taken completely by surprise. Confusion reigned, and the Messengers were powerless. Measures to strengthen Earth's land-based forces had made little headway in the face of human opposition. Even the few nations participating in the defense structure had neither the right nor the means to quell the turmoil taking place beyond their borders. The ET colonies used local energy sources to increase their numbers. Using solar energy, coal, oil, natural gas, and other forms of energy, they built what they required from common, easily processed substances like iron and silicon. Their individual military capabilities were several ranks below those of their brethren in space, who had developed to a much greater level of sophistication, but they were far harder to deal with in groups. They had been bred for effective concealment in the terrain. Again and again, Earth's forces were routed.

After less than two months, the desolation was visible even from orbit. Forests and cities burned, sending huge plumes of smoke high into the atmosphere. Titanic craters, the aftermath of nuclear strikes by Earth's forces, were scattered across the surface. After nightfall, instead of the dazzling city lights that once adorned the planet, an eerie orange glow from vast fires and the stabbing flashes of artillery flickered across the darkened land.

•◆•

"The attack on Mars has begun." Cutty's voice reached Orville at his quarters in the marine city of Penglai, floating in the East China Sea. "The ET are using asteroids in the ten-meter range. No particular advanced weapon use—they probably don't have the resources to fabricate them. Apparently they're using up their last reserves of strength, just as we are."

"Yes. We destroyed their Jupiter bases." Orville's voice contained no trace of optimism. Even if the Messengers and the ET managed to wipe each other out, there would be no victory. The ET were merely weapons, they were not the conquerors themselves. But the Messengers had to fight while exposing flesh and blood humanity to danger, and humanity had sustained a blow from which it would never recover.

Cutty spoke again. "The unit defending Sherwood Evacuation Station in the North Sea has ceased to exist, apparently due to the attack on Mars."

"The attack on Mars?" asked Chan wearily. Chan was the human officer sitting opposite Orville. He had been dispatched by the government of Shanghai to assist Orville and was coordinating the evacuation of civilians to this floating city. Orville answered for Cutty.

"We came from the future. The Messengers in the unit that disappeared were created by someone in that future. That someone had an ancestor in this era. That ancestor was probably on Mars."

"Wait, so that means those Messengers were never created? How is it possible that we knew of their existence? I get it...this one of those time paradoxes," said Chan.

"Our research scientists believe it's possible for us to know those Messengers existed because their existence was imprinted on this timestream when it branched off from the original stream," replied Orville. "Upstreaming time travelers are hybrids—they have attributes of the new timestream and their original timestream—and the relative strength of events and experience in each stream influences how the new stream plays out. You'd have to do a probability analysis based on upstream theory. Don't ask me more, I'm not an expert."

"Don't tell me more, because I didn't understand a word you just said," replied Chan. They laughed cynically. Chan was one of the few from Earth who had been willing to help.

Cutty broke in: "We have the upper hand in space, but the depletion of our units due to interstream interference effects is starting to have an influence. It's touch and go whether we will eradicate the enemy, or whether the reduction in our forces will tip the balance and allow the enemy to replicate back up to strength."

"And even if we do prevail offworld," said Chan, "we can't do a thing about the enemy here on the surface. Correct?" Cutty did not respond. No answer was needed.

Orville downed his tea and stood up. "I'd better get moving. The landing stage at Ningpo should be coming under attack right about now."

"Mr. O, uhm, Orville. I have a favor to ask you."

Orville turned. This was only the second time Chan had used his real name instead of his code name in the month since they had first met. Chan gripped his teacup and spoke in a low voice:

"Is there room for a human passenger aboard one of those ships of yours?"

Orville's eyes narrowed. "I never thought I'd hear that from you," he said stiffly.

"Not me. My wife. She's with child."

Orville froze. Chan stood and grabbed him by the arm with enough strength to make even cyborg bones creak.

"You have room, don't you? Room for one. Some of the ships were fitted out for human officers. For pity's sake...!"

"Protecting your wife is your responsibility," said Orville, his tone reluctant, officious.

"There's no way. It's impossible. We all know that. We can't stop them. This city can't stand up to a sustained attack from their air units. We'll be wiped out. But isn't your mission to prevent that? To save humanity, no matter what? To protect someone carrying new life is consistent with your mission, even if she is my wife. Am I wrong?"

"And if we do take her aboard? What then?" Orville's voice was barely audible. "Where could we take her? Is any place safe? Mars is under attack too. There's nowhere to go. We can't take passengers like Noah's Ark."

"Take her to the past."

Orville reflexively shook himself free. He'd heard enough. He didn't want to be any more coldhearted than he had to be. But as he fled out the door, Chan called after him, his voice full of wretchedness, like some vengeful ghost. "Please, take her with you! Take her to the past, where they can't follow! You can do it. I know you want to!"

As he ran through the streets of this floating city of refugees who squatted, exhausted, in the streets with nothing but the clothes they had escaped in, Orville suppressed the urge to cry out. *Yes, that's right, we're going further into the past, to make amends for this debacle, to start over from scratch. In other words, we're going to turn tail and run. And we're leaving humanity behind.*

He climbed a metal ladder to the top of the wall surrounding the city. A ship jammed with refugees was docking. Another vessel bristling with antiaircraft guns passed on its way out to sea. Far off, a solid wall of black cloud stretched across the western horizon like the peaks of a mountain range. The cities of China's maritime provinces were burning. The low-quality materials used by the land-based ET prevented them from operating in water, but as Chan had said, it was only a matter of time before they overwhelmed the floating cities with mass-produced airborne FET.

Orville noticed he was grinding his teeth. Why were the ET so bent on destruction? What in the world *were* they?

"Assignments for the next Upstreamer detachment have been issued. You're on the list, Orville. Please report to the assembly point. I will accompany you and leave this world to the subunits." In other words, Cutty had also abandoned hope for this Earth. She knew there was no future for this timestream.

Orville murmured mechanically, "Chan's wife, could we take her?"

"Transporting a human into the past is of no utility for humanity. I can't agree to it."

"No utility, but no harm either," said Orville.

"She's not Sayaka. You know that, don't you?"

"Cutty, you—" A howl of fury died in his throat. Orville fell to one knee and began to weep.

CHAPTER 5

Eeeyaaah!

A dozen warriors yelled in unison and charged, a log with a heavy stone lashed to the end carried between them. The ram struck the huge Reaper in the midsection, toppling it end over end. The men drew their swords and pounced, caving in its insectoid eyes and severing the tendons in its legs. Its blue-white metallic body was the first of its type the soldiers had seen. The thing thrashed wildly as it died.

Once it was clear that the beast would never again be a threat, the men turned to seek their next target. Child soldiers, too young to wield the rams, approached cautiously and severed every tendon they could find, one by one.

"A Jumper!"

A single-legged ET the size of a little girl bounded wildly out of the woods, brandishing a thin blade like it was a strip of swirling silk. The blade dismembered men amid fountains of blood. The air filled with howls and screams. A group of soldiers with wooden shields surrounded the ET and hemmed it in. The Jumper kept moving, waiting for its chance, then tried to escape the circle with one tremendous leap, but a toughened warrior seized its leg.

The men surrounded the fallen Jumper and killed it with a frenzied hacking of swords.

A call for help floated up to the ridge from below. A group of warriors were in full flight up the slope. Gaps in the trees behind them revealed another full-grown Reaper. Takahaya called out to them, in a voice loud enough to shake the leaves, "Make for the stockade! We're dropping the sledge!"

The soldiers reached the ridge, stumbling over each other into the stockade. Waiting troops ran past them and cut the rope holding back a huge sledge made of logs, planed flat and lashed together. The sledge skidded down the mountain, sweeping the Reaper with it.

From all directions, bamboo war trumpets had been sounding from watchtowers along the ridges, warning of attacks. Now, one by one, the trumpets fell silent, a sign of successful clashes with the enemy. As Miyo listened from her quarters inside the stockade, Takahaya entered, drenched with sweat. "The enemy is nearly routed in the third valley," he said.

Miyo had stopped using Kan to communicate with her senior commanders. It wasted precious time; moreover, it was no longer necessary to maintain Miyo's aura of dignity.

"Good work. Send reinforcements to North Point and the Tama Cliffs. Help is needed there," said Miyo.

"I sent forty to the cliffs this morning."

"They've been repulsed. Send a hundred more."

"As you command," said Takahaya. Since the beginning of the fighting, Miyo's orders had been prescient. Takahaya left with an air of complete confidence. But her directives were not the result of divination but were instead due to Cutty's comprehensive grasp of the evolving battle lines, and to the Messenger, who fought ceaselessly on the front lines.

When the mononoké made their first incursion onto the plain of Iga, the Messenger went out alone and returned with a small specimen he had captured alive. He bound it to a tree with heavy rope and summoned Miyo's captains. At first, they feared to approach this creature they had only heard about in legend. The Messenger walked up to it boldly, striking and touching it with his bare hands. Even the mononoké were not invulnerable, and their bodies were subject to decay. With the right technique they could be restrained, immobilized, and killed.

After careful explanation and encouragement, the Messenger gave the soldiers swords and cut the ET's ropes. Then he faced the frenzied beast armed with nothing but a fighting staff. The men mustered their courage, attacked, and succeeded in killing the monster. In truth, this ET was in a greatly weakened state, but the men were heartened by their success and swore to follow the Messenger in battle.

The Messenger showed them how to use log rams to topple the enemy and shields for defense. He introduced the wheel and the crossbow. Till then, the Yamatai warriors had relied mainly on bronze swords, polearms, and wooden bows. When the soldiers saw firsthand how a crossbow bolt could penetrate a thick tree trunk at a hundred paces, even their armorers were dumbfounded. Nor was engineering neglected; roads were graded, bridges built; forts sprang up and barriers snaked across the mountains and valleys of western Iga.

The Messenger sent runners to Yamatai, summoning visiting traders and princes from the chiefdoms to observe the conflict, to see how the strange and barbarous mononoké were laying waste to Iga, and how Yamatai's forces were pressing them back. Back in their homelands, the visitors were likely to exaggerate what they saw to their rulers and headmen. This would create far more impact than if Miyo had sent envoys to describe the events taking place. The war with the mononoké had been raging for two months. They had had to improvise, but Yamatai's army held firm as it waited for more than just token reinforcements.

Miyo's quarters stood on a hill overlooking the plain. All around her was the din of an army camp: shouts of men raising log walls, the shrill voices of women distributing food, the bellowing of captains overseeing the training of green recruits, angry demands for quiet from men trying to steal a few moments' sleep. From the mountain at their back came the ceaseless ringing of the woodsmen's axes.

Miyo was visited by an endless stream of messengers, soldiers, and captains. She had only the briefest periods of rest. As shaman, she was used to compelling obedience behind a screen of silence; never before had she been obliged to deliver immediate responses to question after question. Even with the *magatama* providing most of the answers, she was tired of talking and mentally worn out.

When the stream of visitors stopped for a moment, Miyo sent her maidservants outside, sat back, and muttered, "I am weary. I'm beginning to feel light-headed."

"If you don't feel well, I can examine you," said Cutty through the *magatama*.

"You play at healing too?" Miyo shot back, then shook her head. "The problem is my spirit, moreso than my body. Two months ago I'd never have imagined this would be happening. It's like some awful dream."

"Wake up," said Cutty. "This is not a dream. It really is happening, to you and your country. You can't just quit. Still, I must say you're holding up well. Until now there have been so many leaders who were ultimately of little use to us."

"'Of little use'? That's rather harsh," said Miyo.

"Please don't be offended. O rates you very highly."

At that Miyo felt so awkward she could not reply, and when she realized her own awkwardness, she winced. In truth, she'd hoped that cooperating with the Messenger would help her escape from all this. But now she was saddled with a responsibility that sapped her spirit. *What a miscalculation. If only this upheaval could somehow end soon...*

Her mind was wandering aimlessly when cheers of welcome came from the stockade gate. Soon the Messenger's lanky form appeared in the doorway. He sat down, exhausted.

"Forty men lost," he said. "I told them not to go forward so quickly, but I couldn't stop those young soldiers from pursuing the enemy. I should've brought more seasoned men."

"You held the cliffs alone? The reinforcements were too late?" said Miyo.

"They helped all the same. Thanks to them, I got some rest before I came back here. I'm thirsty." One of the maidservants brought a pot of water. He refused the ladle, stood and raised the pot to his lips, gulping water like a stallion. He said to Miyo, "I'm going to the watchtower."

"You're leaving already?"

"Come with me. You need to see the overall situation." They climbed the watchtower on the ridge. The Messenger pointed toward the center of the Iga Plain. "See there? Along the river?"

"You mean where the sunlight flashes?"

"That's the spot," said the Messenger.

"They look like the scales of a fish," she said. The banks of the river bisecting the plain were lined with rank upon rank of greenish panels. Probably the height of a man, each appeared tiny in the distance. They resembled a patch of scabies spread across many acres of tranquil, early summer farmland. Miyo felt her skin crawl.

"Those are solar panels fabricated by the enemy," O said.

"I don't understand."

"Think of them as the mononoké's paddy field. They draw nourishment from them. I don't know what they're doing for energy in Kunu, but it looks like this is the only way they can fill their bellies here. If we can destroy those panels, we can starve them out, in Iga at least."

"Destroy them, then."

"I can't do it alone. That looks like more than two thousand panels, and they're adding more as fast as they can make them. I'd need five hundred soldiers, but we have to protect the borders. We can't spare that many right now. We'll destroy them after we build up our strength here. That's the most urgent objective."

"Once you destroy them, will you reinforce the border crossing further on?"

"No. We can't stop there. We have to push beyond the borders and keep pressing them. We can't stop till we've destroyed the nest. This isn't like fighting a human chiefdom, where you can pause once you've done a certain amount of damage to the enemy. As long as the mononoké live, they can and will replicate without limit. And they'll keep trying to kill us."

"It's enough to drive one mad…" Miyo sighed, but the Messenger's stern expression was unchanged. "Come," he said, and climbed from the watchtower.

His destination was the edge of camp. As they passed, soldiers and peasants dropped to the ground and prostrated themselves before their queen. On the outskirts of the camp they came to a small, jumbled mountain of greenish-white metal fragments, the broken and melted bodies of dead mononoké. Miyo grimaced in disgust. The Messenger hefted a fragment in his hand.

"Right now they're using zinc. That's what this metal is called." The Messenger called to a captain nearby. He handed the soldier the fragment and told him to see if he could shatter it. When the captain placed it on a boulder and struck it with a stone, it broke apart easily.

"As you see, zinc is not a good material for their purposes. Fire weakens it. They're probably using this because they can't get their hands on anything else."

"There are large deposits of this metal in the mountains to the east," said Miyo.

"Then we know where the enemy's stronghold is," said the Messenger. "We know where Earth's mineral resources are located as a matter of historical fact. But the enemy has to do their own prospecting. In that sense, we have an advantage."

"So the enemy, he is weaker than he appears?" asked Miyo.

The Messenger shook his head. "Maybe for the moment. If they can find a source of ore, they won't need to carry out major mining. The ones who need the ore the most will ingest it. The main thing is whether they can reach an ore source. We hold western Japan, with the mines at Izumo, and that gives us the upper hand. But there are huge ore deposits in eastern Japan too, in Emishi territory."

"By the time they reach Kamaishi, the enemy's capabilities will probably be far stronger," interjected Cutty. But Miyo heard this strange new prophecy as if from somewhere far away. She had never heard of the place Cutty named. How the mononoké's power might change because of some different material was beyond her understanding. She felt more and more frustrated. Nothing seemed real.

"Even before they reach Kamaishi, there are small deposits of iron in Chichibu and Osaka. And the other ore fields are not completely devoid of iron. In any case, the longer we wait, the more our advantage slips away. It's no use wishing we were stronger," said the Messenger.

"I see," said Miyo.

As they retraced their steps to her quarters, Miyo struggled to understand the Messenger's words. The mononoké must be destroyed. As long as they drew breath, they would never stop attacking. That they could be destroyed meant they were neither demons nor devils. They were different from the gods of water and wind that the people of Wa had fought for ages without number. They were not like the days, the months, the seasons, which changed and returned in their endless cycles; not like the animals or the insects that might die, yet be reborn from an egg left behind. They were things, things with will, Things That Came. Suddenly, Miyo's hazy images of her old adversaries seemed robbed of substance. She stopped in her tracks. "Messenger O. What are the mononoké?"

He turned and looked at her like a father gazing at a daughter. "That's a very good question. But if you know too much, you might lose hope."

"Have you lost yours?" asked Miyo.

He looked away and muttered, "I don't know."

"Messenger O…" Miyo suddenly felt a surge of anger toward this man who would tell her almost nothing, though she was sure he must know everything. After all, they both shared a common fate. Wasn't there much more he should be telling her? But her thoughts were interrupted by a shrill voice. "Lady Miyo! Where are you?"

"Kan! I'm here!" Miyo waved. The boy ran up, out of breath. He gave a short, almost disrespectful nod to the Messenger and prostrated himself before Miyo.

"An urgent message from the palace. A pack of mononoké has appeared in Isonokami, attacking people and livestock!" Isonokami was only twenty-odd *ri* from the palace. Too close indeed.

"What!" Miyo turned to the Messenger and saw him frown for an instant. "Messenger O? Cutty? What of your vigilance now?" she cried.

"What indeed?" said the Messenger. He hardly seemed

surprised. Would he say something like this was anticipated? No matter. Miyo turned to Kan.

"Summon Takahaya immediately. Does he already know?"

"Not yet," said Kan. "The men are searching for him now."

"Wait, there's no time. Tell him what is happening. I return to the palace. He will accompany me."

"Really? You're going to defeat the mononoké yourself?" said the Messenger.

"You can't come with me, can you?" she snapped. How she might take command of the fighting was far from her mind. She knew only that she had to return at all costs; her desperation spoke for her. But the Messenger just nodded, as if it were only fitting. Kan went to look for Takahaya. Miyo called her maidservants together in a state of distraction. Yamatai, the land of her birth and childhood, burning like Iga? She would never allow that to happen.

• ◆ •

Never more did Miyo rue her inability to ride a horse. She drove her bearers relentlessly, pressing on by torchlight through the night, moving toward the plain of Makimuku with a hundred soldiers handpicked by Takahaya. Even so, the trip took a day and a half.

When they had crossed the last pass and descended into bright dawn over the Shiki plain, Miyo saw the land she had longed for. Rising above the paddy fields that stretched before them was Mount Miminashi, its heavily wooded slopes like an upended cup; on the left hand, Mount Amanokagu and the Yoshino Range. Miyo realized that she had never left this country before. Seeing it upon her return was like seeing a new land.

But there was no time for emotions. Wisps of smoke were rising into the northern sky. The enemy? No, they might be morning cooking fires. Other small plumes of smoke were visible here and there. Miyo could not judge what was happening.

"Permission to send scouts ahead." Takahaya's voice came from outside the palanquin. *Granted,* Miyo was about to say, but then the *magatama* whispered.

"You have arrived? The enemy is twenty-five *ri* to the west—about forty, all RET."

"Can you see them?" asked Miyo.

"The Wasps caught up with them," said Cutty. Miyo had never seen one of these kinsmen of Cutty, but this was not the time to make enquiries. Miyo spoke in a commanding tone through the wicker screen.

"No need for scouts. The enemy is near Miminashi."

"My lady," acknowledged Takahaya.

"Take me to the palace. I must speak with Lord Ikima." Takahaya began giving the orders. As she listened, Miyo thought, *These men can be trusted. They have seen the Messenger in battle and fought the enemy themselves. Yet a hundred of the bravest are no match for forty mononoké. We need more soldiers. But the men from the palace have never seen this foe. Will they break and run?*

With their remaining strength, the slaves carried Miyo's litter over the palace moat at a half-run. By good fortune, the enemy had not yet come this far. But the moment the palanquin passed the gate, a single glance revealed chaos. Everyone was running around as if they'd already been routed, shouldering bundles of clothes and jars of rice.

Miyo could not restrain herself. She lifted the screen, leaned out of the palanquin and roared, "What is the meaning of this?"

The people in the forecourt froze. In Yamatai, there was

only one woman who gave commands. Realizing that their queen had returned, everyone threw themselves to the ground, dropping their pots and bundles with a wave of clattering. One scrawny man emerged from the Great Hall. He seemed to want to prostrate himself, but confusion held him back. He lowered his head, but only partway. He looked up from under and spied Kan.

"Mimaso has no words to express his joy at the queen's return, but if she would conduct a divination to show us how best to flee this urgent danger—"

"You speak of oracles at a time like this? Look at me!" shouted Miyo.

Mimaso sprang to his feet. He kept blinking like a rabbit. He did not know that Miyo had altered protocol completely. His confusion was not surprising, but Miyo had no time for explanations. She began firing questions at him.

"What is all this? Are you running away?"

"I, oh, please, forgive me for speaking directly..." Mimaso blinked again.

"Are you turning tail before you've even closed with the enemy? What are your arrangements for battle?"

"Lord Ikima is in charge. He is gathering soldiers."

"Where is he?"

"He left this morning at the head of his troops," answered Mimaso.

"Where did he go? How many men? What weapons did they take?"

"My Lady, I have been utterly preoccupied since daybreak preparing to leave the palace—"

"Leave it? You should be making ready to defend it, you, you..." Miyo groped for some earthy term of abuse, but she had never used such language and was speechless. In a calmer tone, she gave Mimaso his orders. "Gather every soldier in the palace. Let the women prepare provisions. Children will collect firewood. Stop making ready to flee. The mononoké are to be killed!"

"By you, my lady?"

Clearly Mimaso was going to be of little help. Miyo called to one of the captains and had him assemble his men, but when she saw them gathered together her face darkened. They had managed to scrape together swords and armor sufficient to equip themselves, but most of them were either aged or children—altogether unimpressive. Still, there was nothing to be done. The best soldiers had gone to Iga, and Takahikoné had taken the rest.

It is well that I brought Takahaya, thought Miyo. She was already mentally in command. She called for him and pointed to the men. "Takahaya! Will you slay forty of the enemy with these?"

"It will be a close thing, my lady." The rough-edged fighter from Kumaso ran his gaze over the three hundred men assembled and rubbed his jaw.

"We have some war hammers, but for the rest, only swords and pikes. Not the way I'd like to go into battle."

"We march in support of Lord Ikima."

"Yes, my lady. I'll do my best."

Takahaya had come to Yamatai from Kumaso partly as hostage, to secure the alliance between the two chiefdoms. Takahikoné had showered him with grain and slaves, treating him with cordiality and respect. Perhaps because of this, Takahaya suddenly recovered his enthusiasm. Though he'd hardly slept the night before, he began energetically directing the men to prepare for departure.

Amid the commotion, a war trumpet sounded from the western watchtower. "Fire on the mountain!" Miyo stretched her neck to peer in that direction. Thick, ashen smoke was rising into the sky. This was no cooking fire.

Without hesitation, she asked the *magatama*, "Is the enemy on the mountain?"

"It looks like all the people have fled there," answered Cutty. This did not quite match her question, but Miyo instantly understood the significance of Cutty's reply.

"They're going to burn the whole mountain!" Cutty was silent. Miyo turned to the soldiers and shouted, "Takahaya! We march as soon as you are ready!" He waved in response.

The column set out. Breakfast was rice cakes with chestnuts and dried meat, taken as they left and hurriedly eaten on the march. Mount Miminashi was only six *ri* from the palace, almost within hailing distance. As soon as they were across the moat, the mountain was visible just beyond the river that ran west. Takahaya, riding alongside the palanquin, put a hand over his eyes.

"A large pack of Reapers surrounds the mountain. If they come at us all at once, we'll be finished."

"Can we not trap them?" asked Miyo. Takahaya was about to reply, then seemed to think of something. He wheeled his horse and galloped off to the end of the column toward the baggage train. After a few minutes, he returned. "There is one thing we could try, and I don't even know if it will work. We could lure the enemy, then surprise them with the Hayato."

"A baited trap," said Miyo.

"You should remain here, my lady."

She thought for a moment. "The Hayato for the trap. As for the bait, anyone can go out and make some noise."

"Just so, my lady."

"I will serve as bait. The palanquin is conspicuous," said Miyo.

Takahaya started in surprise, but did not object. "We will pray for your success, then."

After conferring on details, Miyo had her litter brought to the head of the column. With a retinue of only ten, she moved along the embankment road that ran between the river and the paddy fields. The heat in the palanquin was suffocating, but Miyo raised the screens on all sides. Walking alongside, Kan glanced up from time to time with a look of disapproval.

Mount Miminashi drew closer, seeming out of place atop the flat plane of the paddy fields. Then the strange shapes of the mononoké came into view, skulking about the base of the mountain. Thin shrieks could be heard from the flickering fires on the slopes. Miyo gasped.

How many people had been driven up the mountain? Planting was done, but the fields of green rice shoots were deserted. In this season, dozens of farmers would normally be weeding and fertilizing. Naked children should be running and playing on the levees between the fields.

Miyo looked ahead and noticed red lumps scattered across the fields. Suddenly she realized they were corpses. "Butchers," she said, her teeth grinding in rage. Then Kan spoke quietly. "Lady Miyo. They see us."

The nearest mononoké was standing motionless, looking intently toward them, less than two hundred paces distant. Miyo responded sharply.

"Not yet! We must draw as many as possible. Stand fast!" Her bearers closed their eyes in fright and went forward on trembling legs. As she urged them on, Miyo knelt on the floor of the palanquin, braced her back against the roof and pushed. The roof gave way. She tossed the uprights of the litter aside.

As she stood in the sunlight, she looked up at the rock ledge that ran along the top of the mountain. Tiny shapes were visible on its edge. Miyo waved and tried to make them out. She saw the glint of a sword and someone waving wildly, a soldier. He looked somehow familiar.

It was Takahikoné.

He must have gone out to save the peasants and been driven up the peak. A large crowd surrounded him. The flames and smoke were close and getting closer. Miyo could hear screaming and crying.

"Lady Miyo!" shouted Kan. One hundred paces to the base of the mountain. Every one of the beasts was now staring their way. They were probably unable to withstand the fire; nor could they climb the mountain. There looked to be twenty or more.

Miyo took up a war trumpet, inhaled as much air as she could, and blew. A sound like the howl of a huge beast resounded across the fields.

"They come!" shouted Kan. The mononoké leaned on their long arms and rushed forward on all fours, like apes. Kan drew his sword.

There was a scream of fear. The palanquin lurched violently. One of the bearers took off at a dead run. That did it; the other bearers dropped the litter. Miyo was pitched into a water-filled paddy. She felt a flash of rage. "Weaklings!" she yelled.

By the time Kan and the soldiers had helped her up, the mononoké were almost on top of them. They ran. The nearest mononoké did not use the levees but came splashing straight at them across the field. Its scythe flashed and the head of a soldier flew past Miyo. She kicked it out of the way and kept running. "Go!" she shouted, and looked behind her. For a moment she doubted her own eyes.

"Save yourself, my lady!" The remaining soldiers formed a line behind her and held their ground. Miyo stopped reflexively. Kan pushed her forward. "Hurry!"

She ran again. Miyo heard one of her men sounding a deep-throated battle cry into the face of death. She wondered who he was; she realized she didn't know his name.

To Miyo, her slaves, her soldiers, they had generally been nothing more than chattel to her. What a fool she was. If some fled for their lives, others shielded her with their very bodies. All were people, all bound by the name Himiko. But she was only Miyo, nothing more.

The sounds of slaughter behind her lasted only a few moments. Miyo and Kan had run fifty paces on. Again, the heavy drumming of many legs splashed toward them across the field.

"Miyo!"

"No!" she shouted. Kan turned to face the monsters. Miyo yanked his arm with all her strength. Too many had died for her already. She ran, dragging the boy with her. She struggled to breathe. Her heart pounded, her vision darkened, blurred.

It was then that she saw a soldier drawing a bow. "Quick, my lady!" She leapt into the last paddy field. There was a gust of air behind her. She couldn't help turning to look, and one was there. Face to face with a mononoké. Takahaya's longbow sang and a steel-tipped arrow pierced the monster's skull. The mononoké toppled backward into the mud. As soon as they climbed atop the embankment, Takahaya gave the order.

"Burn them!"

Still on hands and knees, Miyo heard the sharp rap of a fire striker, then a sweeping roar. She turned to look behind her and sat down on the embankment.

The field was a sea of flame, burning oil floating on the surface. The mononoké caught in the fire thrashed wildly but made no attempt to escape to the next field. Miyo remembered something the Messenger had told her: the mononoké were able to see heat itself. But because they were so sensitive to it, heat blinded them as if one had thrown a red and swirling blanket over their insectile eyes. Mononoké could not find their way when surrounded by the heat of fire.

Still, about half the enemy had stopped short of the flaming field and were trying to make their way around it. As soon as Takahaya saw them spread out, he gave his next order.

"Attack!"

The Hayato hiding on the riverbank burst over the embankment, screaming their war cry. The enemy was pincered between soldiers and fire. They whirled and used their weapons on the weaker obstacle, the men. Five or six soldiers were cut down, but the rest did not flinch. They gathered around the mononoké, hacking at them and driving them into the fire. The inexperienced soldiers of Yamatai looked on, then joined the slaughter, timid at first but soon fighting wildly.

They were victorious. As the flames ebbed, the piled bodies of the mononoké smoldered in the field and along the levees. Takahaya inspected the battle site and returned to report.

"Twenty-two enemy killed."

"Well done," said Miyo.

"Now we must hurry and deal with the rest." Only the mononoké on this side of the mountain had attacked them; the others remained. As Miyo realized this she stood up quickly, but then someone was shouting, "Look there!"

Battle flags hove into sight at the foot of the mountain. They were long and narrow, not like the flags of Yamatai. They rounded the mountain and moved toward them. Trailing behind them was a force of hundreds. No, more than a thousand. Miyo and the others stared in dumb amazement.

A herald rode forward and stopped before Miyo. "You are from Yamatai? You killed these creatures?" Miyo sensed the need for protocol and looked toward Kan. The boy stepped forward. "Before you stands Himiko, Queen of Yamatai. Who are you?"

"The queen!" The herald dismounted quickly and knelt.

"I serve Inumori, Second Lord of Kunu. In accordance with the covenant of the Laws and by order of Shimako, First Lord of Kunu, I bring a force of twelve hundred to put down the mononoké."

"From Kunu," murmured Miyo. Bringing princes from the other chiefdoms to witness the fighting had apparently had its effect.

"We killed twenty on the other side of the mountain and came to the aid of Lord Ikima of Yamatai," said the herald.

"He is safe, then," said Takahaya with a grin. The herald nodded.

In a few minutes Takahikoné arrived with an escort from Kunu. He dropped to his knees before Miyo. His armor was soot-blackened and split at the shoulder. Clearly he had seen some hard fighting. "My lady, I am filled with emotion to see you here," he said in a hoarse voice.

"Good soldier, you stood fast in defense of people and country. You must be weary."

Takahikoné looked up, startled at being addressed directly by Miyo, but quickly looked down again. Miyo thought she detected a faint look of frustration in his face.

Cries of joy rose from the nearby village. Kan peered in that direction and whispered to Miyo. "The villagers are overjoyed. See how they dance." Miyo looked toward the village. Jubilant at their survival, women and children were hugging each other, dancing and making merry.

•◆•

Miyo was back in the Great Hall of the palace for the first time in two months. She could hear the distant voices of soldiers celebrating in their night encampments. Near sundown, three thousand troops from Toma had also arrived. They brought word that at this very moment, soldiers and provisions were likely on the way from many other chiefdoms.

With noises of celebration echoing faintly in the background, Miyo sat opposite Takahikoné. Lord Ikima's face was dark, and not only because the illumination from lamps placed at either end of the room was so faint. There were black circles under his downcast eyes. His bristly beard moved as he spoke in a low voice. "Queen Himiko—"

"Himiko is enough. When you kidnapped me from my village, I bawled like a child. How long ago was that?"

Takahikoné ignored her invitation to revisit the past. He inched closer on his knees. "Himiko. Then permit me to ask this. Do you really intend to lead the combined armies yourself?"

"Why not? The soldiers can scarcely understand each other's dialects. How can I expect them to follow orders given by the Messenger of the Laws, a man they've never seen?"

"Pray allow me to render this service to you." With stiff formality, Takahikoné bowed deeply. "I would wish that you remain here, to look after the people and perform the rituals. Affairs of war are best left to men. It would be a terrible tragedy if any harm were to come to your person."

"Speak not what is not in your heart, Takahikoné," she answered. "I think the sight of all these troops makes you fear for your position. If I lead the armies, I shall not only win military distinction. If I'm so inclined, perhaps I'll even point my staff at the leadership of Yamatai." She paused and laughed lightly. Then in a voice full of scorn, she continued, "Is that what you think I want? I can barely fulfill my responsibilities as shaman queen. I believe you know well enough what is in my heart."

"That is true." For just a moment, an expression—an honest expression—of wry humor crossed his face. "You hated the very name Himiko, didn't you?"

These things only you and I understand, thought Miyo. She knew only too well what to expect from this man's character. The first time she laid eyes on him, he gave her a glimpse of what was to come. She was only ten, perhaps not even that. She was catching eels with her friends when a man rode toward them along the stream, horse hooves splashing through the water. He was beardless when she'd first seen him. When he learned from the children which of them was Miyo, he glared at her sternly. She would never forget his first words.

"Are you unsullied, girl?"

Miyo was speechless with astonishment. Takahikoné turned to the other children and said harshly, "Have any of you copulated with this girl?"

Some of Miyo's friends were wed at the age of eleven or twelve, but nowhere in Yamatai was there such a debauched custom as indiscriminate sex. Even for someone of his station, Takahikone's behavior was outrageous. The children looked away and pretended not to hear him.

Unfortunately, Takahikoné took their silence as the answer to his question. He suddenly leaned down and hoisted Miyo with one arm. Turning to the children, he shouted in ringing tones, "The oracle proclaims it: this girl will be shaman queen. Go home and tell your parents. Miyo will rule Yamatai!" And so it came to be. Miyo cried uncontrollably atop the violently swaying saddle. She was taken to the palace and handled roughly, like a piece of property. Her parents never saw her again. Not long after, word reached her of their deaths.

Every day was a form of imprisonment. Old Mimaso, her predecessor, taught her the rituals. Every day she performed them, just as instructed. For his success in finding Miyo, Takahikoné was promoted to the rank of Ikima, and arranged affairs as he pleased in her name. Miyo had no shortage of whatever she needed, but her servile handmaidens were under Takahikoné's thumb, and they kept a close watch on her. Often she did not see the sun for days.

If Takahikoné miscalculated, it was because Miyo turned out to have real gifts. As she grew, she acquired an excess of strength and started making all sorts of trouble. Her handmaidens were strict, but only concerning the things Takahikoné had forbidden; they were afraid to use their own discretion for fear of his wrath. Once Miyo realized this, she would refuse her meals, punch holes in the thatch roof, hurl the ritual implements, indeed do anything she could think of that was not explicitly forbidden. Of course, each time she got up to something, it would immediately be forbidden and she would no longer be able to do it; then she would think up some new form of rebellion. By doing so she developed both cunning and stamina.

But by the time she was fifteen she had given up these pranks. She had learned much, and instead of using force to get her way, she began to maneuver the treacherous people who surrounded her into granting what she wanted. Leaving behind a substitute in order to steal outside the palace, arranging for Kan to be her attendant; these were just examples of what she could do with the skills she acquired during this time. Based on her long dealings with the ministers of state, she also realized that as long as she performed her ritual duties, they cared little what else she did. She simply had to avoid doing anything that could damage her authority as a distant object of reverence.

But the greatest incentive for Miyo to conduct herself as shaman queen was Takahikoné himself. His intentions were all too evident. When her monthly cycle began, her breasts and hips began to fill out and she grew taller, her hair long; then Takahikoné began coming to the palace more often. As she felt his sticky gaze, Miyo could not help but remember the question he had put to her on that day she first saw him. Takahikoné wanted Miyo on a pedestal as queen, but he also wanted her for himself.

In defense, Miyo retreated behind the barrier of her authority as ruler. The more formally she conducted herself, the more Takahikoné was forced to withdraw in embarrassment. Until now, this expedient pose had seen her through. Takahikoné knew that if he yielded to his lust he would lose his position. Miyo could feel how this tension, like a bottomless swamp, hung always in the air between them—even here, as they discussed the conflict and the future of the country.

"Himiko…" In the flickering lamplight, Takahikoné again edged his knees closer. Two more paces and he would be close enough to touch her. Miyo stiffened, suppressing the urge to slide backward away from him.

"Keep your distance. You are my younger brother, are you not?" she said firmly.

"That is just a pretense—"

"And you already have three wives. If you leave them behind and go into battle, I'm sure they will be heartbroken." Adroitly, Miyo returned the conversation to its original topic. She looked sternly at Takahikoné, this imposing man near fifty, subserviently kneeling before her. But he was no fool. Quite the opposite; he was calculating above all else. And Miyo knew this well.

"Listen to me, Takahikoné," she said. "You and Takahaya are close. He can guide the armies with a strong hand. I have seen him in battle. I know how loyal this man is. Leave the fighting to him. On the other hand, only you can manage the government. At a time like this the country needs a strong hand. I think you are that strong hand. What say you?"

Takahikoné stared at her fixedly. He blinked, again and again. Miyo almost felt as if she could see through the back of those pupils and into the whirlpool of his brain, weighing the alternatives. Finally he bowed deeply. "Of course. You are right, my lady. I spoke foolishly."

After he withdrew, Miyo was seized by fatigue. Her maidservants entered, carrying trays of food at eye level, which they then set before her. And when Kan entered the room, it was as if the air in the palace had been cleansed.

Attended only by Kan, Miyo reflected on the audience that had just ended. What a waste of time it had been. *The only important thing now is to work out how to defeat the mononoké: who should do what, to increase our strength as much as possible. Yet instead, I must make allowances for this man's ambition, win him over...*

"Lady Miyo, are you tired? Your face—" said Kan.

"What of it? *Your* face is still flecked with today's grime," she said with a laugh. Kan began frantically wiping his cheeks. Miyo laughed. She took a piece of grilled deer with her fingers. Enough with Takahikoné. It would be best to put him out of her mind. Something more troubling was nagging her. Why had the other chiefdoms suddenly begun cooperating now?

The chiefdoms that form the axis of the Land of Wa are suddenly embroiled in a war against the monstrous mononoké. The Messenger of the Laws appears, to smite the enemy. Staking her claim on the Laws, Himiko calls for assistance from the armies of the alliance. And the chiefdoms agree, easily. Was this not truly odd? Even Miyo, with little desire for power, could imagine what the chiefs would be thinking. How many would see this misfortune as an opening to take control of Yamatai and become the new king of Wa? No doubt the fingers of both hands would scarcely suffice to count them.

Still, more motivation than that would be needed. Sending a force of thousands of men was a heavy burden for any country. Yet with the ambitions of tens of chiefdoms to account for, a bid for domination would face daunting odds. Was there anything else, other than a self-interested thirst for power, that would explain their willingness to help?

Suddenly Miyo was seized with a terrible suspicion. Her fingers trembled slightly as she touched the *magatama*.

"Cutty, can you hear me?" Miyo tried to sound nonchalant.

"Yes." The eerie voice answered coolly.

"You certainly made things easy for us today. You'll need more than forty mononoké to really rouse the soldiers."

Cutty's reply went far beyond anything Miyo suspected.

"You finally understand him, don't you?"

"What do you mean?" said Miyo, in complete bafflement.

"You and your people depend on me for so much. But as you see, I am not your ally."

Miyo shivered. Cutty spoke calmly, as if describing another person. "You are quite perceptive, Miyo. I lured the mononoké to Yamatai this time. Just as O showed the soldiers step by step how to fight the enemy in Iga, I sent weakened mononoké to raise the fighting spirit of the soldiers in Yamatai. Think of it as a kind of immunization, a boost for their immune systems. I am doing the same in chiefdoms throughout the Land of Wa. Now you've discovered the truth. O knows of this and he concurs. To rally the forces we need, we must not shrink from deception. This we have learned from bitter experience. We are using you, and by so doing we defend you, and defend humanity."

"Is that what he really wants?" shouted Miyo. "Then I'll never understand him!" Hearing her suddenly cry out, Kan looked up. "Lady Miyo?"

"Wait!" She turned to the bead again. "Did you hear me, Cutty?"

"You misunderstand," answered Cutty. "O would never deceive you for sport. On the contrary, the necessity to do so wounds him deeply. But since we learned its necessity he's deceived countless people, used them, sent them to their deaths. Because of this—no, in spite of this—the guilt he's carried with him since he started on this journey grows stronger. It is the remorse he feels for not abandoning the larger mission of saving the species just to help those in immediate need."

His guilt? As Cutty's words sank in, Miyo was overcome with a painful dizziness. It would be as if she had abandoned Kan to the mononoké to help spring the trap. And this the Messenger had done, again and again?

Cutty's voice betrayed the hint of a smile. "I am Cutty Sark, witch of artifice. I brandish the mare's tail, I am the guide on the swiftest path to victory. I use whomever and whatever suits my purposes. The winds of time scatter all. The sands of time bury all. The winds and sands have battered no one more than Messenger O. If anywhere there were a woman who could sustain him, I would make quite sure that she did. But in a thousand centuries there has been no such woman."

"Lady Miyo!" Kan was shaking her shoulder. Miyo woke from her reverie. The boy was holding a cup of water and peering at her with concern. "You look so pale. Perhaps you should rest."

Kan was so kind. Single-mindedly devoted, always ready to sacrifice his life for her. Losing him would be more than Miyo could bear. She embraced him and held him fast.

"My lady?" Kan's body stiffened. The cup slipped from his hand. After a few moments, Miyo pushed him away and stood up.

"Where are you going?" asked Kan, still dazed.

"I need solitude."

Miyo climbed one of the watchtowers and asked the soldiers to leave her. The light from the encampments gave the palace a festive atmosphere. Beyond stretched the endless paddy fields, glistening in the moonlight.

For the first time, Miyo truly realized that she ruled this land and understood how much she loved it: the mountains, the fields, and Kan and Takahaya who lived there, and others like them, nameless soldiers and peasants. Not until they were threatened did she grasp their true value. Toward the person she had been, a girl dreaming of running away at the right opportunity, she felt nothing but contempt. With that realization, the weight of her responsibilities, the terror of wondering how in the world one could possibly accomplish what was needed, hit home.

She looked eastward. Beyond the Kasagi mountain range looming darkly before her was a man. A man who felt the same burden.

"Messenger O—how did you bear it?" She had much to say to him.

Chapter 6

Unmarked Stuka dive bombers and Shturmovik tank busters took off from their base in the Finnish north and thundered across the frozen wastes. One after another they rose into the sky in groups of four, eight, sixteen planes; they fell into precise formations and banked toward the northwest where the escort fighters waited high in the sky. Unpainted, silver-bodied P-51 Mustangs; Bf 109s in the Luftwaffe's white-and-brown winter camo; and Macchi C.202 Folgores, their tails striped green, white, and red. National markings were officially banned, but as usual the Italians had ignored the regulations.

Oulu was a small Finnish town that had been turned into a huge military installation. Over five hundred aircraft were bound for the enemy's base at Kiruna. Allied ground forces were already pushing toward the Swedish iron min-ing complex. After nearly losing Europe, humanity had finally succeeded in cornering the ET. The air campaign would strike the death blow to the enemy in the Northern Hemisphere. Their colony at Fushun had already been annihilated by the Chinese Communist Eighth Route Army. Pockets of ET resistance in Australia and South Africa were under fierce attack from the Anglo-Indian Imperial Fleet and the Imperial Japanese Army and French ground forces based in Indochina.

For their third encounter with the enemy, the Messengers had chosen the height of the twentieth century's largest and most sprawling armed conflict. The goal was not simply to change the course of history by taking advantage of a vast military buildup that otherwise would have been wasted in intraspecies warfare, but to intervene at a point when humanity's readiness for armed conflict was at its zenith. Arriving on Earth four decades into the twentieth century, the Messengers succeeded in convincing the world's nations to set aside their conflicts and prepare to fight the ET. They used everything from pressure tactics to discrete manipulation of public opinion. When the fighting got under way, humanity proved it could defend itself. It seemed certain that total victory would be theirs within a year.

And yet, Orville was not happy. A fellow Messenger, one named Quench stationed in Washington, told him:

"Listen, Orville. I have some bad news. The Americans can only spare four carriers for the recovery operation."

"They promised six."

"Right," said Quench. "And now they're diverting two of them to South Africa. You'll have to make do with four."

Orville felt the frustration rising again. Most of the planes dispatched from Oulu to Kiruna could not carry enough fuel to return. The plan was to have them land on U.S. carriers off the coast of Norway. Six carriers would barely be enough to recover all the planes. With only four, the planes would have to refuel and take off again immediately. Orville doubted that the German and Soviet pilots could manage it. They had neither the aircraft nor the training for carrier operations.

"Why are they doing this to us? Their own fighters are participating in the mission," said Orville.

"Yes, but the Mustangs have a range advantage. They can make it back on their own. What I'd like to know is, what's the White House up to? It sounds like they're planning to grab some of the credit for the British victory."

"What's the point of antagonizing Churchill?"

"Our agents in Berlin report that Roosevelt and Hitler have a secret agreement. They're already looking beyond the end of the war. Our closing of Auschwitz seems to have had some unintended consequences," said Quench.

Orville sighed. This was becoming a pattern. Behind the façade of global cooperation, multiple conflicts were poised to boil over, conflicts even deeper than those from the original timestream. The Second World War was inevitable given the conditions that preceded it. Now Earth had united against the ET, but the old antagonisms continued to fester beneath the surface.

Cutty Sark had long been pushing for a complete takeover of Earth, but the Messengers no longer had the power to seize the planet. Less than five percent of the Upstreamer Forces that left the twenty-sixth century remained at their disposal.

Orville was deep in thought as he walked toward his quarters in the Allied Air Command Center. Since the arrival of the Upstreamer Forces, a succession of Messengers from alternate timestreams had begun arriving in this era. The Messenger Orville had just finished speaking with was sent by humans of the twenty-fourth century. But the Original Messengers had no record of them; these Descendant Messengers owed their existence to changes the Upstreamer Forces were making to history. With support from these new Messengers, now might be the time to take some bold action. He decided to contact Cutty.

"Can you talk?"

"What is it? I can't spare much time."

"Still got your hands full?" He waited.

"Things are very dicey right now, Orville. Can it keep?"

"Talk to you later, then," he said. The slight delay in Cutty's response was due to the distance between Earth and the Moon, where her ship was located. ET from the twenty-second century had also reached the Moon and were trying to establish a foothold. Orville terminated the comm. Cutty indeed had her hands full.

The North European Allied Air Command was composed of generals from the four powers, along with officers from countries providing logistical support. When Orville announced the shortage of carriers, the exchange of sour looks began immediately. It was grimly humorous to see the surprise of the American general, who had been kept in the dark by his superiors, but Orville was in no mood to enjoy it.

After a few moments of silence the usual furious arguing broke out. The Soviet and Italian generals criticized the Americans; the U.S. commander reminded them of America's risky strategic bombing operations from the British Isles and insisted on equal sharing of the burdens of war. The German general pretended to be neutral while discreetly supporting America, as if his superiors had already notified him of the secret German-U.S. deal. The French and Spanish officers, officially just observers, began stoking the argument. Orville pounded the table.

"Wake up, people! We don't have time for this idiotic squabbling!"

Everyone turned to stare at him, some with hostile expressions that seemed to ask a single question: *Who got us into this mess in the first place?* The American general went on the offensive.

"What about the Upstreamer Forces? You must have some strike capability, or am I wrong? What was all that talk about reinforcements arriving every day? Just propaganda?"

Orville was silent, and let the silence be his answer. In a moment he was forgotten and the generals had gone back to fighting amongst themselves. Earth knew all about the arrival of the Descendant Messengers. As Orville and the Original Messengers pushed the ET back in 1943, history itself changed, increment by increment. People survived who would have died; technology that would have appeared in later eras became possible now. This in turn accelerated the development of AIs. Then mankind looked to its past and upstreamed Messengers to critical eras to provide support.

Logic dictated that the number of Descendant Messengers should keep rising as enemy losses rose. The destruction of a single ET generated a new timestream. Humanity in this new daughter stream would be in a better position to develop AIs and send them into the past. With the enemy's final defeat, all barriers to technological development would fall, and humanity would be able to create as many AIs as desired. They would seed the past and the future with multitudes of AIs, and their own timestream would be absolutely secure against further attack. This was the true significance of the arrival of the Descendant Messengers. It was also the Upstreamer Forces' ultimate goal.

But things were not working out as planned. The new Messengers confirmed that humanity in their timestreams had advanced significantly. But for many reasons—social, economic, and political—these timestreams had not reached the point where they could assemble a significant temporal army. This pointed to one conclusion: entire temporal universes were on course to extinction.

But there was something else the Messengers were withholding from mankind.

Several months previously, the number of newly arriving Messengers had started dwindling. At the same time, they were arriving from farther and farther in the future. The most recent arrival came from the year 2680, even later than the Original Messengers. That meant that humanity's capacity to create AIs was emerging later and later in history. Cutty's conclusion was that the Upstreamer Forces' interference in events was becoming counterproductive, actually slowing the progress of the species instead of accelerating it.

Orville had seen nothing wrong with actively changing history. What would be the point of minimizing interference if the result were the loss of humanity itself? He had no desire to create more tragedies like the one that befell Chan and his people. He no longer cared about nations or cultures. All he wanted was to help individuals survive. But painful as it might be, experiences like this demonstrated how wrong he was. Those looks of suspicion! As soon as the ET were mopped up, it was clear that these men would once again divide their world into enemy and friend, creating endless conflict.

Orville turned his back on the bickering officers and stepped outside the command center. He stared vacantly at the vast, snow-covered runway and muttered, "What do they expect us to do?"

"Hey, Orville, got a minute? I want to ask you something." The cheerful voice on the comm link was Alexandr, his data tag marked Singapore. He was an advisor to the Japanese army at their frontline command center.

"I'm all out of resources, Alex. I shipped the Komet aircraft you requested. I don't have ground forces to spare. The rest of the French army has to stay put in Algeria," said Orville.

"No, it's not that. My bear needs some lackeys to carry out his dirty work. Any ideas?"

"Your bear?" Orville sputtered in bafflement, his emotion

translated and carried through the comm. "What's that, a code name for the Russians?"

Alexandr chuckled. "Come on, don't play games. You told me to put a bear in my story. You know, for the villain."

"Yes, maybe I did, but..." Orville recalled that short conversation with Alexandr on the surface of the Moon. It had happened a few years ago in their frame of reference, but it was actually 180 years in the future. A human might have forgotten it, but short of major damage, Messengers retained every microsecond of their experiences.

"You actually decided to use a bear?"

"Of course. Bears are like guardian gods of the forest. So why does this one want to kill the tree? Come on, you gotta find out, right?" said Alexandr.

"Maybe he went crazy."

"Oh, the motivation isn't important. I just want to grab the reader's attention. So how about those lackeys?"

"I don't know. What about crabs?" It was a shot in the dark. Orville had crab each morning with his Finnish breakfast. Alexandr slapped his thigh.

"Of course, crabs! Crustaceans with bright red shells, crawling around deep in the forest. It's got impact. Yeah, the bear tells them to crawl out on every branch and snip the leaves off, one by one. It sounds scary. No way can those little caterpillars fight off these crabs, even if they all join forces."

Orville was silent. "So things are bad, eh?" said Alexandr.

"We're at a very difficult juncture," answered Orville.

"I have no idea how we're going to defeat the ET."

Orville suddenly felt a nasty foreboding. "Have they come up with something new?"

"This says it all," said Alexandr. He transmitted an image to Orville's visual system. It was a black-and-white photo with a superimposed grid, taken from the air. There was a barren plain scattered with boulders, and at the upper right, a tiny white dome resembling a parasite. Judging from the grid scale it might have been five meters across. "A Mitsubishi Ki-46 observation plane took this over Mount Bruce in western Australia."

Was it an enemy structure? Orville had never seen anything like it. "It's not a nest," he said, half to himself. "No hatch, no generator. What is it?"

"I didn't know either, so I sent Wasps to image it from different angles. Here's what I got." Alexandr sounded proud of himself. The next transmission was a false-color thermal image. Orville was stunned. The dome now sat at the center of a series of concentric circles up to a hundred times as large, seemingly floating in the air.

"Geothermal energy transmission. That dome has roots that go fifty klicks straight down, sucking up heat. It can generate four or five hundred times more energy than they need for replication. They could even upstream without relying on antiprotons."

"Nuke it," said Orville impatiently. "I'll send you a warhead from Peenemunde right now. Singapore, right?"

"Now hold on," said Alexandr. "This is where it gets really interesting. We found 139 of these silos. What you're looking at is the last one we found. And except for this one, the rest were already empty." Orville could feel his legs bucking. He leaned against the wall of the command center.

"That's just in the Southern Hemisphere," said Alexandr. "I think they've been spotted in your half of the globe, too. You could check it out, but it probably doesn't matter." He was laughing, a sarcastic, dismal laugh.

The Messengers had always assumed that the ET would rely on solar energy. Now the enemy was almost cleared out of near-Earth space. The rest were planetside, not an ideal place to be dependent on solar energy. The resource war, and thus the initiative, had seemed to favor the Messengers. But if the ET were using geothermal energy, the rules of the game had changed dramatically. The amount of power they could access at any time would be far larger. Aerial detection would be difficult. It was almost as if the ET had switched over to guerilla tactics. If they used the energy they harvested to keep upstreaming, all of mankind's past would be in danger.

"Why are they doing this?" Orville wailed. After all, the enemy were only machines. Yet their sheer doggedness suggested that they were not just obeying some program. Who or what was behind them?

"Based on the depth of each silo, a rough calculation of the amount of energy available allows us to estimate how far they can upstream. We're already working on that. When we get the answer, we'll be leaving too," said Alexandr.

"So we can go from branch to branch, knocking off the crabs."

"See? You do get it. I'll have to add tons of caterpillar friends to the story so they'll have a fighting chance. Damn, the subplots are going to get out of control. I wonder if Shumina will read the whole thing."

"Maybe not till you finish serializing it. Who knows, maybe the ending won't be happy," said Orville.

"Don't say that!" Alexandr sounded back to normal, which made Orville feel more like himself too. "Have you notified Cutty?"

"Of course, but she's totally occupied," said Alexandr. "I wonder what would keep her from dealing with something this important."

Just then Cutty joined the conversation. "Sorry to keep you waiting. I am returning to support mode. I was trying to crack a very difficult cipher. The enemy made a transmission from their communications hub. By laser to Teegarden's Star, twelve light years from Earth."

"Does that mean we were wrong about where they came from?" Alexandr asked impatiently. But Cutty's response was glum.

"Teegarden is a red dwarf. We wouldn't expect to find intelligent life in its vicinity. In the twenty-sixth century humans had an unmanned observation station on one of the planets out there—it feels strange to talk about this in the past tense, doesn't it?—but all it detected were some chemically synthesized bacteria."

"But the ET wouldn't beam a message to an unoccupied location," said Orville.

"Correct, so this is still an open investigation. And I haven't broken the cipher. There is insufficient data. But your discovery is quite important, Alexandr. I just searched our database of images from the Northern Hemisphere. It appears there are more than 400 silos worldwide."

"Then we need a new strategy," said Alexandr. "If the ET are going to upstream without limit, we'll have to match them. But there's also a limit to our numbers. Why don't we take a page from the enemy's playbook and start self-replicating?"

Orville was shocked by this proposal. "If we started using self-replication, we'd end up overwhelming the human race. Don't forget, our mission is to *serve* mankind."

"That's true," said Cutty. "And there's no advantage to dividing our forces. Instead of chasing after individual ET across multiple timestreams, we should upstream farther back in time and defend the future from there."

"You say 'farther back in time,' but how far do we go? The enemy has the initiative," said Alexandr.

"I have a plan," said Cutty. "Original and Descendant Messengers, please join us." Cutty opened the conversation. Messengers all over the planet now heard her voice.

"First, I'm sending you the data on Alexandr's discovery. Has everyone received it? Then here's my analysis: the enemy has acquired the capability to upstream without limit. Logically, they could travel back to the root of this timestream and inflict damage on Earth as it was several billion years ago. However, I doubt they will do that."

"Why?" said Alexandr.

"Because if the damage they inflict takes place too far in the past, it won't influence the human species. Biological evolution is highly adaptive. Given enough time, even the effects of extensive damage can be overcome. Of course, the new evolutionary path may yield humans that are not primates or even mammals. But the concept of parallel evolution should apply across branching timestreams. Therefore, the best way to retard the progress of humanity for the longest possible period is to inflict damage as close to the present as possible. The enemy knows this."

"You must have an idea where they will strike."

"I believe the most critical, vulnerable period for mankind is the point at which modern humans are just emerging as a distinct species. Therefore, we must go back a hundred thousand years, to the African savannah. There we defend the species to the death, with all our forces. We draw a defensive line and prevent the enemy from upstreaming any further."

"I'm not impressed by your logic," said Orville. "What defensive 'line'? We can't create a physical barrier. Is there a technique to prevent the enemy from upstreaming wherever they want?"

"There is no such technique," replied Cutty. "What I

propose is merely a plan of action. We upstream a hundred thousand years, settle in, and maintain a vigil until each breakaway group of enemy finds us. Then we eliminate them piecemeal. It's inconceivable that they could upstream that far in a single jump."

The network fell silent. A thousand centuries? Was it really possible to defend a span of time that long?

"Of course," Cutty continued, "our hardware was not designed for such extended deployment. We will use cryostasis technology to extend our operational lives for as long as possible." This last remark failed to lighten the stunned atmosphere hanging over the network. Cutty casually added: "We will hold a referendum on this plan in sixty seconds. If anyone has objections or questions, now is the time."

There was silence for forty-five seconds. For Messengers, with their high-speed language and powers of thought, it was like a human year. But on the forty-sixth second, Alexandr spoke. "What an idiotic plan, even if it is the best we have. Cutty?"

"Alexandr."

"My story is going to be so long, no one will read it."

"I'll abridge it for you."

"I'll do it myself," he said, signaling agreement to the plan. A few of the Messengers laughed. In seconds, the votes started coming in. In ten seconds, the ayes topped 50 percent. A few moments later they approached 90 percent. The voice of Cutty cut in. "Then it's settled."

"Wait. I'm out." It was Orville.

"And may we know the reason?" Cutty said.

"Mankind will be wiped out downstream of every era where the enemy stops off in the process of finding us."

"True. Streams without us in their past—this stream, for example—will be abandoned. Ultimately it will be as if they never existed. Indeed, they *will* have never existed, like a decision left unmade. We will defend all timestreams generated after our arrival one hundred thousand years in the past."

"Not possible," said Orville. "Do you know how many streams we will generate in a hundred thousand years?"

"Perhaps you can tell me. I do not care. My mission is to secure a single timestream for humanity to be safe from attack for all eternity."

Orville shook his head. "I'll defend the timestreams you propose to abandon. When I'm finished, I'll upstream and rendezvous with you a hundred thousand years B.C.E. It won't affect your combat strength."

"Defend mankind against ET scattered across more than four hundred timestreams! And how will you do that?" Cutty snapped. The network buzzed with murmurs of astonishment. Orville muttered, "That's my problem."

"I'll go with him." Several voices rose simultaneously. Orville realized one of them was Quench. He wasn't surprised. Quench owed his existence to the Original Messengers' efforts to push back the enemy.

Twenty-four Messengers volunteered to join Orville. Cutty was silent, apparently deliberating. Orville pressed his advantage.

"I'm telling you, by the time we rendezvous, my Messengers will have accumulated experience from thousands of enemy engagements. And if we manage to create some productive timestreams, more Descendants might join us."

"This initiative of yours will affect our combat strength," said Cutty. "It requires another vote."

The results stunned Orville. More than 90 percent approval—it might have been 100 percent had the Messengers all voted with their guts. Cutty sounded resigned. "You are hereby authorized, but you will also take one of my subunits for support and to document the action. The subunit will be installed on your weapons."

Document the action? I can do that myself, Orville was about to object, but he kept silent. He knew what Cutty was up to.

"I now close this conference. Please upstream once you complete your current task. If you do not have sufficient energy, my assembly point is London. I will descend and pick you up."

As the buzz of discussion faded away, Orville found himself once more enveloped by the silence of a snow-covered landscape. Even the occasional plane taking off and landing was strangely muffled.

He sat down on a discarded ammo crate. In that vast quietude, memories of Sayaka came welling up. Even now he could remember every word of every conversation they'd had. That is what it meant to be an AI. But with the passage of time, the very concreteness of the data seemed to make the reality of what he had actually experienced, of how his body had responded to her, harder and harder to hold on to.

Sayaka cherished loyalty to humanity. He had been moved by her conviction. Yet they had never come to a conclusion regarding what was most precious. For Orville, in this time and place, the notion of defending the ocean of history, that gigantic system of endlessly branching timestreams, had been replaced by an almost heartbreaking mass of details. Each tributary on each stream cut through the bedrock of the universe thanks to the power and flow of human experience. Given the attention it deserved, no one drop was more or less valuable than another. Cutty Sark ignored individuality; her formidable analytic mill reduced everything to abstractions. He felt an unbridgeable gulf opening between them.

If Sayaka had met Cutty, what would she say? Images of her, of those intense conversations with friends that lasted till dawn, flooded his mind. She never yielded an inch of ground to anyone. Yes, she and Cutty would have struck some serious sparks. Both aimed at something that was the same, yet crucially different. Was it really only a matter of the collective, the species, versus the interests of the individual? Or was it about something far more important?

Orville was overwhelmed with longing. When he had held Sayaka's lithe body, the truth had always seemed so obvious. But that was in the past, in a time yet to come, a future that would never come. Like snow gleaming on distant peaks, it was gradually sublimating, vanishing into the aether.

"Cutty Sark is pretty cold-blooded. Do you trust her?" Quench's matter-of-fact voice put an end to Orville's musings. He rubbed the stubble on his jaw as he brought himself back to reality.

"No. Cutty's very capable. Anyway, commanders are like that. The subunit is probably to make sure we don't start a rebellion."

"What a dictator," Quench groaned.

"That's how they made her," Orville replied calmly enough. "No use complaining. We Messengers were made to focus on individuals. Cutty looks at the big picture. Our designers thought of everything."

In Quench's silence, Orville sensed that the other Messengers might have come to a decision. Finally Quench spoke. "Those of us who are going with you consider you our leader from now on. Everyone's agreed."

"I'm on Cutty's blacklist now, you know," said Orville.

"Doesn't matter. We're on it with you."

Orville gave a bitter laugh. "Suit yourself."

"Original Messenger!" said Quench. "We await your orders."

"Assemble in London. We have to pick up the subunit, and I want to meet all of you in person." Just then a young pilot walked past. Orville recognized him and waved him over. "Listen, when's the next flight to London?"

"London?" asked the pilot. "No direct flights, but that Messerschmitt Gigant is leaving for Oslo in twenty minutes." The enormous six-engine transport at the edge of the runway was taking on cargo. Orville had never seen one of these ungainly aircraft. He looked it over with interest.

"I'd be happy to fly you personally. You'll want to reach your destination quickly, I expect."

Orville looked at the pilot. His left hand was bandaged; he'd been wounded a week before, when the transport he was piloting had been attacked by FET. Now he was grounded. If Orville named him pilot, he could return to the air, even somewhat handicapped as he was. There were few opportunities to win distinction flying transports, but Orville knew he was one of their best.

"Then I name you pilot, Hartmann. Get your orders in the command center and report back."

"Jawohl!" The youth's face glowed with pleasure. He saluted and took off at a run. It was a sight Orville would never forget.

CHAPTER 7

By the time the Yamatai forces reached central Japan, eight thousand men had fallen.

Miyo herself led the armies in three major battles, Takahaya in eight. His captains led the troops in thirty or more smaller engagements, and every day brought short, sharp clashes with Jumpers and flying Red Snipes that harried the columns all along the march. The Eastern Sea Road, later to become the main artery between Edo and Kyoto, was still just a weed-choked path. All along its course, the armies shed casualties and a rain of discarded armor and weapons. Not a day passed without burial ceremonies for the dead.

The fighting at Toyokawa was a bloody affair. Just as the Kunu messenger had warned, they found that the fan-shaped plateau extending from the foot of the mountains was so thick with wriggling Kappa and Centipede ET that the ground was hardly visible. The base of the tableland was ringed with waiting Reapers and Jumpers.

The Yamatai forces opened the battle with hundreds of huge darts fired from Scorpio catapults, a weapon from far-off Roma. Until the Messenger taught them the techniques of construction, they had known of this weapon only by name.

Equipped with steel armor and swords, the Yamatai armies charged the waiting Reapers. Eight hundred yards to the rear, in her palanquin, Miyo heard the low rumble as their lines collided. She saw dead soldiers hurtling through the air like dolls, streaming blood. Thunderous explosions sent columns of greasy smoke into the sky above the battlefield. Crossbow bolts glancing off the enemy glittered in the distance like spray in the sun.

The line was contested for hours, until the dead lay in heaps. The Messenger was always in the thick of the fighting, his great sword slashing in all directions until the ground around him was strewn with twisted metal. But it was not the Messenger who decided the battle's outcome. It was the Emishi, whose lands had been stolen by the mononoké. They broke the enemy line after a suicide attack that claimed more than half their men. Miyo seized the opportunity and sent her small force of cavalry to strike the retreating foe. This marked the end of the Reapers. The small green Kappa and many-handed Centipedes were poor fighters and were cut down by the thousand.

When the armies reached the forest atop the plateau, they discovered round stone structures like forts on the rocky ground. The nests of the mononoké. They were extremely tough—even with war hammers the men could not break them down—but the entrances to the nests were open. The men poured in water and oil, tossed torches into the openings and sealed them. Soon the nests erupted in towering pillars of fire. The explosions were violent, incinerating the soldiers who stayed too close to the nests after delivering the oil and torches.

After the battle came the Wasps, the size of dogs, droning over the battleground on transparent wings. These kindred of the Messenger were keen lookouts in the sky, but they could not fight. They landed and examined the ground with their feelers, looking for small black fragments of metal to eat. They had a taste for the bodies of young mononoké. It was said they would not harm people, but no soldier dared approach them.

After the straggling Reapers and Jumpers had been dispatched, the men smashed the remains of the nests. They had completed their trial by fire acquiring the combat techniques they would use in countless future engagements.

In their camp near Lake Hamana, Miyo saw a map of Japan for the first time in her life. "This is the Land of Wa. The shaded area is ocean, the white is land," said the Messenger.

They were in a pavilion guarded by soldiers. The Messenger's brush sped over the silk as he drew the map. The shape that emerged was like nothing Miyo imagined, extending diagonally across the cloth from upper right to lower left. It resembled some sort of creature. Miyo looked up at the Messenger, perplexed.

"I don't recognize this island. Where is Kunu? Or Yamatai?"

"Kunu is here, on this plain. Yamatai, in this basin here."

"What, is Yamatai so small?" asked Miyo.

"The island is huge. To the east lies the largest plain in Wa and the biggest iron mines." It was not just the shape of her country Miyo had never seen. The lands beyond Kunu were shrouded in mists of uncertainty. Nothing was known of their geography or the names of those places, or about the relationships between chiefdoms—which were friends and which were foe. She did not even know how far to the east the land extended. She could only listen like a child and try to remember the place names the Messenger taught her. The journey to Lake Hamana alone had seemed long enough to reach China. When she thought of the distance that lay before them, she felt close to dizzy. "The Land of Wa is so vast."

"If that's what you think, I'd better not show you a map of the world. You'd faint. Roma and Kentak are a hundred times farther."

"One hundred!" exclaimed Miyo. The Messenger smiled. Miyo leaned toward him. "You have been to other countries, yes? You've seen Roma and Kentak?"

"I have," said the Messenger.

"Tell me about them." Kan brought cups and a beaker of sake. He turned to go, but Miyo stopped him. "Kan, you should hear this too, about the lands beyond."

"But my lady…" Kan feared it would be presumptuous.

"Don't be so formal. The Messenger's tales are always better with an audience. Isn't that right, O?" The Messenger said nothing, and Kan seemed unconvinced. Nonetheless, Miyo tugged the boy's hand and made him sit. The Messenger took up a cup.

"Shall I tell you about Kentak, then?"

"Yes. Please."

"I arrived in 1863, to intervene in the North-South War and destroy the ET." The Messenger began his story. Miyo had heard many of these tales since the armies embarked on their expedition. Each began the same way, with an unknown era in an unknown land.

"At that time, Kentak was part of a country called America, where the white-skinned peoples had taken over from the red-skinned tribes. The country was divided into whites who held the black-skinned slaves by force, and other whites who were opposed to slavery."

"They wanted to kill the slaves?" asked Miyo.

"Kill them? No, they wanted to free them."

"Then what? Would they abandon them?"

"They assumed the slaves could fend for themselves," replied the Messenger.

"How heartless," said Miyo. "Slaves would die without their masters."

"People in the north of that land thought it would be better for the slaves to die than to be worked like beasts."

Miyo quietly poured the sake for Kan. Although Kan disliked the Messenger, he always found these tales from other times and places enchanting and strange. How could a country get along without slaves? There were curious lands indeed on the other side of the ocean. Yet as Kan the slave found himself stressing the indispensability of slaves, it occurred to him that there was something odd about it all, though he could not say exactly what.

"Well then, did you fight to free the slaves?" asked Kan.

"No. I told you, I was pursuing the ET. Slavery did not concern me. In fact, I used the slaves against the enemy. I roused them and sent them out to fight. And many of them died, among the seven hundred thousand who fell from North and South. Maybe there were more. Toward the end the situation was so confused I couldn't keep track. Perhaps by trying to help, I only made history worse than it would have been."

"And you joined with people in that era to fight, as you do here?" asked Miyo.

"Yes, I did." The Messenger suddenly seemed at a loss for words. He looked up into space. Miyo waited, thinking she might hear the names of those he had known. But finally he shook his head. "They all perished."

"You lost?" said Kan. Miyo glared at him, but he took no notice. He was gazing at the Messenger.

"It's not as if you killed them," said Miyo. "In fact there

must have been some countries that fell before you were able to help."

"Japan, in 1710," said the Messenger. "It was the Genroku era. They simply did not have the strength to fight the ET. I had barely gotten them organized when Honshu was wiped out, then the three other main islands. The Satsuma clan managed to hole up in the Ryukyu Islands, but there was no way we could win. In the end I had to withdraw."

"Where is Japan?" asked Miyo.

The Messenger smiled. Miyo rarely saw this vulnerable, relaxed expression. Even when he laughed, he rarely opened up like this, and never when conferring with his captains or urging the men on.

Wherever he went, thousands were caught up in his exploits. The harder he fought, the more men died. Mountains of dead and oceans of blood marked his path. Expecting him to shed tears when recounting these horrors was useless. He must have lost the strength to cry long ago.

For Miyo it was the same. Since leaving her homeland, she had seen nothing but death. The soldiers guarding her palanquin seemed to change daily. These men, whose laughter and quarrels she heard through the wicker screen, were like chestnuts being fed into an enormous mortar, daily broken into pieces.

She ordered them to fight. She ordered them to cut down anyone who tried to run away. All she could do in return was to promise to make each day's burials as lavish as possible. And still they obeyed her. They heard again and again that their homes would burn if they were defeated, and seeing the ruined villages along the way, the men faced the enemy with a boldness that startled their leaders.

Miyo noticed Kan was nodding off. She sent him away. Now she was alone with the Messenger. "Aren't you going to turn in, Miyo?" he said.

"I should ask the same of you," Miyo replied. He gave her a sharp look of concern. Then he gradually seemed to understand, but shifted nervously in his place on the dais. "So you haven't been sleeping either," he said.

"No. There are too many ghosts," said Miyo.

"I'm sorry I pulled you into this. You didn't have to be here. Lord Ikima should have come in your place."

"I'm not sorry. It's given me the chance to know you."

"I'm not worth knowing," said the Messenger.

"Really? I would know you more." Miyo felt her pulse quicken as she took his hand. It was a huge, muscular hand with tapered fingers. He recoiled in surprise, but she gripped his hand tight and placed it against her breast.

"You don't have a wife, do you?"

"No, but..."

"I know," said Miyo. "You promised yourself to another, and you intend to return to her one day. But when will that be? Ten years from now? A hundred? A thousand?" Miyo tugged on his arm but he did not move. Instead she drew herself toward him. "Is this woman so important that you would wait alone for a thousand years just to spend a bit more time with her?"

The Messenger turned away. He was staring at his other hand. "This hand remembers her. This remembers that human form, how it felt. That's the basic difference between me and Cutty Sark, a difference my makers granted me. If I forgot about Sayaka, it would be like forgetting who I am."

"O..." Miyo had feared these very words, but on actually hearing them, she felt her strength draining away. Her cheeks burned with embarrassment and anger at being spurned for another, yet she could hardly deny his feelings. But as she began to withdraw her hand, he gripped it harder. "Miyo," O said. He looked at her, his faced etched with pain. "I can't go back."

"What?"

"I'll never go back. We've changed too much history. Sayaka's timestream is buried under the far reaches of eternity. The odds of her being born again are a hundred billion to one—no, even less. There's no way I could ever reach her now. My memories of her are all I have, but even my memory isn't immune to the passing of time."

He clasped her roughly, holding her with a fierce strength. Passionately he whispered the name of a stranger in her ear, over and over. Just as passionately, Miyo suppressed the resentment she felt rising within her. O had carried this burden for far longer than she could imagine. He had abandoned his native land, knowing he could never return.

She exhaled deeply, releasing the tension in her body. If necessary, she was ready to be his lost lover. All she wanted was to bring this man some measure of peace.

"O, tell me your name. Your real name."

"My name."

"Let me call you by your true name."

"Orville."

"Orville," she repeated. For a moment the Messenger shuddered violently, as if an electric current had passed through him. He began to weep uncontrollably. Miyo struggled free, then embraced his powerful body again.

•◆•

From that night on, Miyo and Orville shared the same bed. Neither of them spoke of it, but they did not tell their attendants to keep it secret, and thus it soon became widely known. Miyo worried for a moment that the morale of her troops might be affected, but her fears were groundless. The pairing of a demigod who wrote the Laws of the Messenger with the shaman queen who served the gods and spirits was not so surprising; the armies seemed to think it augured well. Gifts of meat and fruit from the soldiers arrived each day.

The Yamatai armies left Lake Hamana strengthened by twenty thousand men from the western chiefdoms. They were now a huge force of thirty-seven thousand. They also heard rumors of aid, soon to come, from a great chief who held sway over the far lands facing the northern ocean.

They pressed on, encountering many unknown chiefdoms of the Emishi. Most had been ravaged by the mononoké and were now resigned to their doom. The Yamatai forces took the survivors as slaves or slaughtered them as enemies. And still the armies crept forward, like the kudzu vines that spread across the land.

As they headed east, summer turned to autumn. It took them a day to round the smoking, savage cone of Mount Fuji. That night was cold, and at dawn the next morning they saw the mountain crowned with silver. Above the soldiers' heads, geese and swans called stridently as they crossed over, enormous flocks flying now high, now low in the sky.

As the armies neared the Sasago Pass, the peak of Fuji, dyed a mysterious blue, towered above them in the distance. In a fierce ambush, the troops lost several hundred soldiers and many veteran captains. Takahaya came to their aid immediately, pursuing the mononoké through the pass and destroying them with overwhelming force once on open ground. But Orville looked grim as he watched the Wasps pick over the battlefield.

"Has something gone wrong, O?" asked Miyo.

"I don't know. Maybe I was wrong about where they've built their stronghold." He said no more, but was clearly worried. Late that night, hordes of Wasps, more than anyone had ever seen before, droned across the sky, heading east.

Orville led the armies down onto the huge plain of Musashino. The vast flatland was covered with rushes, small groves of trees scattered here and there. Along the coast lay a few Emishi villages. The land was overrun with tens of thousands of deer that had never seen a hunter, along with huge numbers of fox, badgers, and weasels.

Scouts were sent to the top of any rise in the ground. They built towers to survey the land, but haze obscured the northern mountains. To the east, they could make out a vast, shallow lagoon fed by a huge river. The lagoon was covered with what at first seemed to be white fog or haze. On closer inspection they realized it was flocks of migrating cranes and swans.

Takahaya was not happy in this new terrain. He murmured to himself, "I don't know how we're going to defend ourselves in this country." His fears were justified. The armies were hauling huge catapults, and the baggage train extended for many *ri*. Defending this huge collection of men and pack animals would be difficult when the plain offered so few natural defensive positions. Takahaya was nervous and repeatedly sent cavalry to reconnoiter. But the enemy was almost disappointingly few, numbering only an occasional Red Snipe. After three days' march, the armies went into bivouac in the lee of a small, beach-rimmed cape called Atago Hill.

That evening, Miyo climbed the hill in search of Orville, who had still not returned from an earlier errand. He had opened his heart to her in their camp at Lake Hamana, and they had become still more intimate since. But when they entered the plain of Musashino, he had donned his warrior's armor. Miyo was unsettled.

"Why are you so anxious? There probably isn't a mono-noké within a hundred *ri* of this place," said Miyo.

"That's what bothers me," Orville replied. He peered into the dark. His vision was keen even on starless nights. "If I were the enemy, I'd lure us out onto this plain and surround us," he said in a low voice. "Our supply lines are stretched to the limit, and winter will be here soon. It's the perfect time for them to strike. Why don't they come?"

"They must be hiding in the mountains," said Miyo. "You said yourself that they like the metals they find there."

"Perhaps. Or they might be planning a flanking move from the north, down the Nakasen Road. But I raised cairns in that direction. We've been keeping a close watch and we've seen nothing."

"Could you send Wasps?"

"I already have, but the air from here to Kofu is full of FET. They make it hard to do good reconnaissance."

"The Snipes never leave us in peace," said Miyo, her voice defeated. "Red Snipes" was the name the men had given to the flying ET. They posed little threat to the armies and few took them seriously. But FET did target Orville's Wasps, and they were victorious more often than not.

Orville was silent for some time, deep in thought. Suddenly he said, "We should build a settlement here."

"You mean stay the winter?" Miyo was astonished. Orville nodded.

"Withdrawing now would not be wise, and I don't like our dependence on pack trains from the west for provisions. Game is plentiful here. We could even plant grain and bring the women from Yamatai. The men could settle down, gather stone, fell trees, and fortify the settlement."

"You would have us stand our ground here till next year?"

"Next year or the year after, until this land is fully under our control." Miyo's eyes widened in surprise. "Do you miss your country? You can go back. It's all right with me," he said.

"You're not serious." Miyo glared at him, but Orville just laughed. It was a strong laugh, full of warmth.

Next day the armies began the laborious preparations for overwintering. Men were sent out to cut down trees. Hunters fanned out in all directions in search of deer and boar. Those whose nagging injuries kept them from seeking game went to gather wild fruit. A stockade was raised, moats were dug, and a storehouse for grain was built. Every female survivor from the villages in a hundred-*ri* radius was brought to the camp. Then the wives and children of the older soldiers began arriving from Yamatai. The fortress of Atago began to take on the features of a town.

Orville sent out Wasps and scouts, not only over the plain but to Hitachi and Shimotsuke—even as far as Iwaki in the northeast. But the country was empty except for deer and other wild animals.

"Maybe the mononoké died out? Maybe only the Snipes survive, and only because we cannot bring them down." Kan's unsophisticated surmise even started Cutty deliberating seriously, but she decided there was not enough data to reach a conclusion.

And so autumn passed peacefully into winter. The stockade and moat were completed three days after the first snowfall decked the plain with white. Then the last supply train arrived from Yamatai, and the fortress gate was closed.

That night, the enemy came.

•◆•

Miyo's dreams were cut off by a detonation that rocked the ground beneath her. She sprang up, fumbled with her tunic, and raced to the door. The next instant Orville was by her side. A red flash lit the sky. The north gate of the fortress splintered under an exploding shell. More shells rained down on the north side of the fort. The building rocked with each impact.

The instant Orville saw the explosions, he groaned in despair. "Cannons. They've got artillery!"

"What do you mean? Is the fire another mononoké?" said Miyo. Orville said nothing but went to get his sword. Cutty's rapid-fire updates poured from the *magatama* bead. "Warning, artillery detected. Fifty units, large-caliber, ballistic. Explosive projectiles. Ground troops detected five hundred meters from the north wall. Fifty...eighty...one hundred twenty ETs. Thermal stealth—no, low-temperature cloaking. The enemy are disguised as animals!"

"I don't believe it," said Orville. "The Wasps would see right through that. What about magnetic and sonic scanning?"

"Sonic scanning is limited by Wasp wing beats. Apparently the enemy's sonic signature fell below that limit. Magnetic scanning is ineffective in this area due to the geology."

"What, metal deposits on a floodplain? No way. The ET must have seeded the area!"

"In that case we have a real problem, O. You built your fortress in the center of the spider's web."

"Enough! There's work to do!" shouted Orville. He ran, cursing, to meet the enemy, sword in hand. At last the war trumpets began to blare from the watchtowers. Stunned soldiers poured from their quarters, struggling to don their armor. Miyo shouted to Cutty, "I'm sending troops to the north. Is that where they should go?"

"Keep the men well dispersed. The shells—" Cutty's voice disappeared in the roar of a huge detonation. Miyo was blown off her feet. The world spun around her, then the ground came up. She lost consciousness.

•◆•

She did not know how much time had passed. It might have been seconds or hours. Her ears were buzzing. She could hear the frantic screaming of the slaves, the shouts of the men, and even Cutty's voice, but everything was strangely muffled. She had no idea what was happening. Then someone slapped her lightly on the cheek.

"Lady Miyo!" Kan's voice was hoarse. Miyo opened her eyes to find him bending over her, his face streaked with tears. Gradually her senses returned, but each was sending the same message: pain. Miyo shuddered as the agony took concrete form. Kan was distraught. "Where does it hurt?"

"Everywhere. Help me up." As she sat up, she tensed her arms and legs and tried to move them. She could not raise her right arm. She turned toward her shoulder and just as quickly looked away. The bones must have shattered. Her shoulder was deformed, her back scorched. She must have been thrown clear of the building and struck the ground. She grabbed Kan with her left hand. "Don't touch my right side, I tell you! What happened?"

Instead of answering, he looked over Miyo's shoulder. She turned to see her quarters reduced to a pile of burning debris, as if a volcano had erupted beneath them. "A fireball struck," said Kan.

"Where is Takahaya?" Again Miyo's words were cut off by an explosion from another part of the stockade. A wail of despair came from one of the watchtowers. "The sea wall!" A great shout rose from a thousand throats. Soldiers streamed past them, racing to defend the opening in the wall. Miyo shouted to Kan through the din.

"Where is Takahaya? Where are the catapults?"

"I don't know," Kan shouted back. "I came as soon as you were hit."

Three more explosions. The northeast tower toppled slowly, like a tree felled by loggers. Battle cries and the ringing of swords came from all directions. The war trumpets blew wildly. Captains bellowed at their men. Soldiers ran toward their assembly points, others wandered in a daze. It was perfect chaos. Miyo shouted into the *magatama*, "Where is the enemy's main force?"

"All around you," Cutty replied quietly. Miyo sagged with shock. "Just before the attack, thermal signatures of deer and boar were detected encircling the compound," said Cutty in the same dismal tone.

"How many?"

"Three thousand seven hundred." Just then a roar of voices rose from the eastern ramparts. Bloodied soldiers came streaming back from the line, shouting in panic, their swords ruined, some nothing more than shards . Slow-moving Reapers loomed behind them in the smoky darkness. In the light from the torches their bodies were rust red, clearly different from before. Miyo remembered the first of these beasts that she had seen up on the mountain, and how its unyielding body had broken Kan's sword with ease.

"It's just as I feared. They found the mines at Kamaishi." It was Orville.

"Messenger O?" Miyo strained to hear him through the *magatama*. He was gasping for breath. It sounded like he was in the middle of combat.

"They're using iron catalysis to make gunpowder—that puts them a thousand years ahead of us. It's no use; we can't fight this. You've got to give the order to withdraw."

"Withdraw? After all our work?"

"We need reinforcements from other countr—" The word was swallowed by a scream.

"Messenger O!" Miyo shouted. All she could hear was Orville panting as he grappled with some foe. She looked toward the north. Beyond the smoldering stockade, the rumble of explosions sounded like the foreshocks of an earthquake. A mass of burly Hayato warriors rushing with log rams pushed forward to repel the ET advancing into the fortress. Takahaya was there, and he turned and shouted to Miyo. "Queen Himiko! You must flee!"

"Push them back, recall your men, and prepare to withdraw!" Miyo shouted in reply. She stood up, but a wave of agony from her shoulder nearly brought her to her knees. Instantly Kan was beside her, lifting her onto his back. "Give the order, my lady. I will bear you." Miyo nodded and shouted for all to hear, "Men and women of Wa, to the west! Follow your queen!"

Perhaps the counterattack had been somewhat successful. The shells stopped falling. People emerged from their huts with everything they could carry. The Hayato ran ahead to the west side of the stockade, to repel the enemy who would be waiting there.

"Messenger O, we leave through the west gate. Join us, quickly," said Miyo into the *magatama*.

"No. I have to hold them here, otherwise they will follow you."

"Orville!" cried Miyo fearfully, but the Messenger laughed. His voice was suddenly dry, like a summer wind. "Spare me the histrionics, I've got my hands full. I'll follow you as soon as I can."

"I'll be waiting!" said Miyo. One of the Hayato brought over a horse. Kan jumped into the saddle, and the men helped Miyo climb up behind him.

"You can ride?" she asked with surprise.

"I've learned," he answered in a low voice, and drew himself up with pride. Miyo realized his voice was finally starting to break. He shouted, "Open the gate!"

The enemy stood lurking in the darkness just beyond the light of the torches. A barrage of fire tore the gate apart. The Hayato ran forward, screaming their war cry. Miyo held tight to Kan and the boy spurred his horse.

•◆•

Of those who had crossed the Sasago Pass that autumn, just over half made it back to the west side. From there they marched to the sea, where Orville finally joined them. But soon the enemy, far stronger now, caught up and hit them hard. Very few of the men Takahaya fed into the maw of that terrible machine returned alive. Stripped of their catapults, tormented by hunger and cold, the armies retreated, leaving a trail of the sick and the dead like grains of rice trailing a torn sack. Orville's Wasps could not approach an enemy equipped with firearms. High in the sky over the dwindling armies of Yamatai, the enemy FET circled in dismal swarms, like the great birds who fed on the bodies of the dead in far-off Maya. By the time the armies reached the snow-clad shores of Lake Hamana, their numbers had shrunk by more than two men in three.

"Well, we can expect no help from China," said Cutty. The Yamatai forces were now gathered by the lake, in more of a bivouac than a defensible encampment. The snow fell heavily.

"The Western Jin Empire sent four hundred thousand to fight the ET in northern China. Messengers from Lishan Station are assisting them, but the situation on the ground is not developing to our advantage. The battle in East Africa is shifting toward Lake Victoria. The enemy forces are increasing rapidly. Messengers in cryostasis at Uluru Station in Australia have been urgently mobilized to deal with an ET communications node I discovered on Mount Bruce."

Miyo glanced at Orville and looked away. He had become terribly gaunt. His armor, which he now wore night and day, was riddled with holes and cracks. It was a wonder he wasn't badly injured. Or was he?

"O, are you all right?"

"I heal quickly," Orville replied. He emptied a large cup of sake in one gulp, but this only increased Miyo's concern. She took his hand. "You must rest. For one day, or even one night."

"Rest? No. This is one war we can't afford to lose. We've reached the end of the road," he said.

"But couldn't you go back into the past," said Miyo, "and try again?"

"It's not that simple," Cutty interjected. "This entire conflict has reached a turning point. For the last thousand centuries we have consistently frustrated the enemy's plans, sweeping their fragmented forces off the map of time before they can replicate past the point of critical mass. If they defeat us here, their numbers will grow exponentially. The advantage we've enjoyed until now will be gone. Then the ET will upstream and destroy us where we first appeared in the past. But..." A new tone crept into Cutty's voice. "O, has it ever occurred to you that we could automate the upstreaming process into an endless loop?"

"Don't even think it!" Orville shouted. "Another hundred thousand years of fighting? Give up everything we've won so far, and keep doing it over and over till we get it right? Maybe we should just redo evolution from the beginning! What a load of crap." He hurled his cup across the tent.

"We would have to build an antimatter plant," said Cutty, as if she hadn't heard him. "Our energy supplies are dangerously low."

"That's why we have to finish this here, in this timestream," snapped Orville. "We have no choice."

"Naturally. After all, there's Miyo to consider," said Cutty quietly. The color drained from Orville's face. "Miyo is here, so you cling to this stream. Isn't that correct?"

Orville recovered his ability to speak after a long moment.

"Cutty, are you malfunctioning? What are you talking about?" He spoke slowly, with a hint of menace. Cutty's reply came in a voice nearly devoid of expression.

"It is time for me to reevaluate our strategy from the ground up. I may have to carry out a full-scale retreat and reorganize our forces. If necessary, I can travel to multiple star systems, building strong points along the way. To do this, I will require all the antimatter in this timestream. That includes the antimatter that now powers the Messengers."

"You'd fight on alone?" said Orville. "And sacrifice all of us in the process?"

"There is that option." Cutty's voice was like ice. "If reinforcements from the future fail to appear, I'll create them myself. Everything depends on how things develop in this timestream."

"Go ahead and try it," Orville said. "I'll warn every Messenger and see that you're destroyed."

"How interesting, since I have a kill switch for each of you."

Miyo could not bear to hear more. "Stop it, both of you! What about the Laws? Where did they come from, if not from you? How can we stop the mononoké unless we join hands and combine our strength?"

Cutty and Orville fell silent. Kan's voice came from outside the tent. Miyo told him to enter, and his head appeared at the tent flap. After a long look at Orville, he finally spoke, his voice downcast, "The messenger from Yamatai has returned. Lord Ikima says he cannot send us further provisions until spring."

"How unfortunate," said Cutty. Miyo glanced sharply at the *magatama*. Cutty was an AI. Doubtless the statement was meant to be taken at face value. Yet the hint of sarcasm was unmistakable.

There was a rumble like thunder in the distance. Another explosion. Orville grasped his sword and stood up. Miyo clutched at him. "Wait—"

"I won't be long," he answered. She looked up at him. He was wearing the inscrutable smile she had not seen for months. A tired smile, one with nothing left to hide.

They could hear Takahaya now, rallying his men. Miyo's right shoulder was throbbing. Orville had used another of his mysterious techniques to treat her injury, but she discovered that accelerated healing brought heightened fever and pain. Yet Orville suffered physical trauma almost daily. How much pain had he experienced? How much of his strength had been used up simply to recover?

Miyo stood and followed him out of the tent. She resolved never to speak of her pain again.

CHAPTER 8

Across endless skies, dark thunderheads drifted slowly, like vast floating castles. Two sharp lines of footprints, large and small, ran along the bank of a stream, impressed deeply into the volcanic soil. They had been there for millennia, and would endure for millennia to come.

Another set of footprints was strung out along the streambed, left by the heavy boots of a tall, gaunt biped.

"Cutty, do you read me? It's Orville. I'm back."

"Welcome, Orville. Your return raises our combat strength to 97 percent of its 1943 level. So you made it after all."

"Four hundred and six timestreams, 370 defeats. Combat strength, 4 percent," said Orville. "I'm the only one left."

"Then I celebrate your survival and mourn the dead," Cutty said. She fell silent, but Orville could feel her presence, like a ghost in the network. He heated the tip of his sword and carefully carved a resting place in the volcanic soil for the personal effects of his fallen comrades, including Quench.

"I have your combat log from my subunit. This is just an estimate, but your efforts saved the lives of roughly twenty-six billion people across all timestreams. Congratulations."

Orville winced. Was she being ironic? Then again, she did have a fondness for figures. Maybe she *was* genuinely impressed.

"Shall I brief you now? Or would you like to rest for a few years first?" she asked.

"Brief me now."

"Hold on, Cutty." It was Alexandr. "I want to know what the wanderer's been up to." It had been centuries since Orville heard that familiar voice, though for Alexandr only six years had passed. His voice was filled with respect and affection.

"Messenger O! Congratulations on returning in no more than one piece. Now tell us all about your adventures."

"This says it all," Orville answered dryly as he transmitted his combat log.

"Oh come on, Orville. I want to hear your version."

"Are you running out of story ideas again?" Laughter codes began streaming in from Messengers listening on the network. Alexandr sounded embarrassed. "I'm always looking for good ideas. But that's not the only reason."

"Well, it's good to be back. But there'll be plenty of time to compare notes later. Right now I'd like to know the situation. The enemy could show up at any time."

"Duty first. I see you haven't changed. All right, here's the situation. Africa is our stronghold. Our early warning net covers the planet and everything from here to this side of the Moon. Here's how our forces are deployed..."

The Upstreamer Forces' main base was on the shores of giant Lake Victoria, near the Great Rift Valley. Cutty Sark had used every asset at her disposal for its construction. There was a small mining operation and factories for producing everything from Wasps to weapons. Their overall strength was little more than a shadow of the great armada that left the twenty-sixth century. It was not even equal to the military power of Germany in 1943. Still, their base was Earth's strongest fortress at this point in history.

Living near this nexus of advanced technology that had suddenly appeared were scruffy-looking animals, wandering hunters of game and fish. Their most distinctive feature was their bipedal gait. When the other Messengers took Orville to meet the creatures who would one day be their makers, he was frankly disappointed. But as he observed them at the lakeshore by day and in their camps at night, he began to feel the same affection he felt for their descendants.

Homo sapiens idaltu had only a few hundred words to describe their world. They were warlike, preoccupied with finding mates, perpetually short of food, fearful of the dark and of sudden storms. But they had the compassion to share their surplus game with weaker comrades and the courage to stand up to dangerous predators. They asked endless questions in their primitive language about everything Orville did, the objects he carried, his dress and his body. Humankind's boundless intelligence and curiosity were blossoming before the Messengers' eyes. As he remembered the achievements awaiting their descendants, Orville's spirits gradually began to recover.

Shortly after he arrived, Cutty finished scanning Earth for traces of the enemy. Had she enough Wasps and satellites, such a survey could have been carried out in less than a month, but it had taken her six years. At the same time, the Messengers' global network of cryostasis facilities, constructed deep underground in geologically stable locations, was finally complete. The Messengers dispersed and went into suspended animation, waiting for the call to action that was certain to come.

The enemy attacked sporadically. Sometimes they attempted to build secret nests, sometimes they sent units of full-grown

ET to wreak havoc. Earlier hominids had long before migrated as far as China and Southeast Asia, but small colonies of these "old ones" from the first exodus out of Africa still existed. The ET were drawn to them, distant as they were from the Messengers' main base, and the attacks hastened the extinction of these ancestors of modern humans. But Cutty soon located the intruders, and whenever she sounded the alarm the Messengers would awaken and eradicate them, usually without much difficulty.

The Messengers had resolved to interfere as little as possible with history, knowing how large the impact could be at this crucial stage of human development and over such a long span of time. But there was no way the newly evolved, impressionable human brain could fail to be influenced by the close proximity of entities from an advanced civilization.

The first sign of this influence was the sudden emergence of settled farming communities fifteen thousand years earlier than expected, and in Ethiopia rather than Mesopotamia. Around the same time, a hardy band of Africans from the second exodus succeeded in crossing the Bering Strait and founded a huge, thriving kingdom in North America. They penetrated as far as the tributaries of the Mississippi and into Kentucky, where they were the first to build large wooden structures and make extensive use of the wheel.

Later, the seagoing Phoenicians sailed forth from the eastern Mediterranean and succeeded in making an audacious crossing of the Atlantic. This created links between the Old and New Worlds thousands of years before history as Orville knew it.

In the South Pacific, knowledge of the healing properties of tropical plants spread widely, and the discovery of a certain antimalarial fungus enabled humans to settle in large numbers in New Guinea. These people became master builders of huge stone structures, and in their giant oceangoing vessels they created a far-flung ocean empire extending thousands of miles, from Peru to the east coast of Africa. Instead of leaving behind a scattering of enormous structures before mysteriously disappearing, they seemed destined to become one of the principal civilizations of mankind.

As culture advanced, so did the art of war. There was no way to change mankind's propensity for conflict as a way of settling problems, but the Messengers intervened discreetly when they could. They created and disseminated a code of laws, the central theme of which was that disaster is part of the fabric of the world and is certain to come. Only those who join forces and work together will stave off calamity.

As the centuries passed, the enemy's forces seemed to grow. The number of Messengers lost in battle increased, as did the ranks of those who abruptly disappeared when the timestream that originally created them was rendered extinct. Given the vast changes taking place at the very founding of human civilization, this impact on the future was inevitable. Orville had left his footprints across so many timestreams that his existence was secure, but many other Messengers were not so fortunate. At the same time, the number of Descendant Messengers failed to increase. Perhaps this timestream was destined for extinction? Or perhaps future humanities in other streams considered the implications of technology before blindly pressing forward, even forsaking the creation of AIs.

Whatever the answer, the Messengers no longer had any way of knowing. They had plunged too deeply into the labyrinth of time and could no longer gauge the magnitude of the effect they were having on history.

Around 1000 B.C., Egypt's New Kingdom replaced Phoenicia as a regional power in the Mediterranean and became the target of a major enemy offensive. Alexandr was advising the Egyptians when the ET attacked. Orville rushed to the Nile Delta with the army of Aksum, whose huge empire stretched from Ethiopia south to Mozambique and Madagascar. Together the two Messengers engineered another enemy defeat.

They celebrated their victory on the terrace of a magnificent villa overlooking the receding floodwaters of the Nile. The six great pyramids on the Giza plateau loomed across the great waterway. Alexandr was describing his latest ambition—placing his huge, handwritten manuscript in the great library at Alexandria when it was finally built—when suddenly Cutty's voice came on the network.

"I bring you news, Messengers. Nearly a hundred millennia ago, soon after we arrived in this timestream, I launched a small probe toward Teegarden's Star. I couldn't spare antimatter for propulsion, so I used a solar sail. Twelve light years! The probe took 72,000 years to cover the distance, and for 25,000 years it orbited the star, waiting. But patience has finally been rewarded. I have a message from the creators of the ET."

"No. You're joking." Alexandr was stunned. "How?"

"It was a group of upstreamers from their world, 120 million years in the future. You were right, Alexandr. Teegarden's Star will be their home planet, but not for millions of years.

"These beings achieved control over their own evolution through chemical synthesis of living cells. When they acquired the ability to travel back in time, they began surveying the past. Among their discoveries was the fact that their home planet was nearly rendered unfit for life in our twenty-sixth century, after the intervention of an alien life form: humans. The construction of our observation station nearly destroyed the primitive microbes that eventually evolved into their ancestors. Therefore they decided to take revenge."

Orville cut in, baffled. "Revenge for something that happened millions of years before they evolved?"

"You cannot judge them from the standpoint of life as we have experienced it. They are not oxygen-breathing humans or even carbon-based life forms. They experience the world in a different way. But we can still understand something of their motivation. If those primitive humans by the shores of Lake Victoria were indiscriminately slaughtered, how would you react, Orville? So the ET creators sent a time army to execute a preemptive strike on humanity. An army of self-replicating, self-directed fighting machines."

Orville nearly cried out. "That means our twenty-sixth century was not the original stream. It was a branch created by wars with the ET!"

"Yes. And now we know why our attempts to contact them failed. They did not want to be contacted."

Orville felt the weight of thousands of years of bloodshed pressing down on him. It was too much to absorb.

Alexandr's voice was hoarse, "They didn't want to be contacted. It was all a grudge. This is what they call justice. And you say they're a different species? They're more human than we are!" He began laughing hysterically. Orville was too overcome with fatigue to stop him.

"What were they doing in the past?" Orville asked Cutty.

"They came to destroy my probe, of course. But I anticipated this. The probe was designed to pose a series of questions before they could destroy it, to allow it enough time to complete a diagnostic scan. Was it truly necessary to destroy Earth in the twenty-sixth century? Why did they use weapons of such surpassing cruelty? Why did they deploy their forces across so many timestreams? They snuffed out ten times more lives than you saved, Orville. And the lives that never came to be? A hundred times as many. And finally: Were they satisfied with the results?"

Orville felt a kind of despair. How many lives had the Messengers themselves cast aside to save the species? What was the difference?

"Perhaps these were more like denunciations than questions," Cutty continued. "But as I hoped, they were provoked, and they chose to respond. 'Revenge must equal the damage done, or it is not revenge. The velocity of our evolution was contracted by twelve million years as a consequence of your meddling. Twelve million years of delayed evolution is the price of our revenge, and it has not yet been fully exacted.' There was just enough time for a burst transmission from the probe before it was apparently destroyed. The message took twelve years to reach me."

"So we wait a thousand centuries to talk to them, and they spit in our face," said Orville.

"They told me what I needed to know." Cutty sounded strangely elated. "Don't you see? If we destroy their home planet, final victory is ours. Or we can threaten to do so, if they refuse to come to terms, although I think a negotiated settlement would be extremely difficult."

"Chances of success?" asked Orville.

"Unknown, for both options. A fully armed time force would be required to implement this strategy in any case."

"Then everything we've done has been for nothing."

"But that's not all," said Cutty brightly, ignoring Orville. "The enemy's actions confirm once and for all the effectiveness of attacks carried out via upstreaming."

She's falling apart, thought Orville through a haze of indifference. At the outset of the mission, Cutty had been capable of an almost human capacity for nuanced thinking. Later, she had evolved a sort of cold-blooded stubbornness. And now she was manifesting this eerie elation. It reminded him of a certain kind of tyrant that he had found fairly common across history. Of course, her responsibilities were overwhelming and she had no one to turn to for support. But Orville felt no sympathy. It might even become necessary to fight on without her. Maybe she had even considered that possibility herself.

Alexandr looked up and snapped his fingers near his ear, the Messengers' signal for a private talk. Orville nodded. They switched to a secure frequency.

"I was almost up to five thousand pages," said Alexandr.

"What? Ah, right. Your story is twice as long as when you and I rendezvoused in Laetoli."

"Well, here's a preview of the next chapter: the caterpillars are going to secrete a special sticky fluid in a ring around the tree. That will keep the crabs from digging down and cutting the roots. After the crabs are defeated, they visit the old rhinoceros beetle that lives in a hole in the tree, and he leads them to a jewel he hid down in the tree's roots when it was just a sapling. The jewel gives off a mysterious light, and the ants use it to heal the tree's wounds."

"Alex, that story of yours is a masterpiece. The crabs cut the leaves off the tree and kill their insect friends, and the caterpillars swear revenge. Amazing."

"Yes, it all comes down to the bravest of the caterpillars. Their journeys from branch to branch create so many interesting subplots."

"I loved the battle where they rally for a last-ditch defense of the tree's roots and use webs to trap the crabs."

"I was pretty proud of that chapter myself. I got goose bumps writing it. I'm the author, but I couldn't wait to find out what was going to happen next."

Alexandr's magnum opus had attracted a devoted readership among the other Messengers during its hundred thousand years of gestation. His eyes shined like those of a child when he talked about his saga. Orville smiled as he listened to his old friend wax enthusiastic over the latest installment.

"When the caterpillars at last reach the place where

the taproot divides, final victory is within their grasp. If they can win this one, the power of life will return to the tree, and it will be able to shake the crabs off its branches by itself."

"But what would the bear say?" interrupted Orville. "The bear is behind this whole war, but he just stands by watching. He doesn't say a thing—until now. 'We didn't start this. You caterpillars are to blame. We used to sleep in that tree, and everything was peaceful till you came and started feeding on the leaves and took it over for yourselves. So we'll show you what it feels like to have your home taken away.'"

Alexandr looked deflated. He sighed deeply. "Children's stories don't have to have a moral."

"Listen, Alex. How long have you been working on this? Your story is too big for a children's tale. With a little revising this could be an epic fantasy saga, like the *Mahabharata*. Why don't you give it a try?"

Alexandr stared reproachfully at him. "Have you forgotten who I'm writing this for?"

"No, I haven't forgotten," he said. He gazed at his friend with compassion.

"If I start making revisions now, Shumina will never be able to sort things out."

"Do you still think those capsules are going to reach her?"

"Of course they will!" For a moment Alexandr was indignant, then he lapsed into silence.

Orville looked up at a sky of beaten brass, colored as it was by windblown sand. He lowered his eyes and saw a beautiful young girl in a white toga feeding fish to some pelicans that had landed in the villa's reflecting pool. The girl caught Orville's gaze and waved gaily.

"Why did Cutty tell us all that just now?" Alexandr sat chin in hand, as if pondering a deep philosophical question.

"Maybe because she just found out?" said Orville.

"I wonder. I think the timing was deliberate. Smelling salts for the troops. She's worried we're losing our will to fight." He closed his eyes and furrowed his brow. "She reveals who the enemy is, their goal, and exactly how to defeat them. I think she knew it was past time for us to hear this."

"If she's making it up, or if she's been sitting on it, waiting for the right timing, we could easily find out. But assuming it's true, what do we do?"

"It's simple: go back to the twenty-sixth century and do the job right this time. Oh, I forgot. We can't go back. After everything we've been through, I'm afraid Cutty still doesn't understand much about motivation."

Orville laughed bitterly. "I don't care what she has us do next. As one of your readers, I just hope you'll be able to write the epilogue."

"Tell that to the bear."

One of the pelicans flapped its huge wings, splashing water over itself and the girl. Her laughter was like a tiny silver bell. For just a moment the mist created a small rainbow, framing her like some river nymph. Alexandr gazed at her, and finally smiled.

"Is she a slave?" asked Orville.

"Yes. The pharaoh thinks I'm the reincarnation of the god Horus, so when he gave me this villa he threw in a 'child of Ra' as a bonus."

"Can she read?"

"Not a word, which is too bad. She thinks my pages are for blowing her nose."

The girl ran up onto the terrace. She crossed her wrists over her breast as a mark of respect to Orville, then began talking excitedly to Alexandr and tugging at his sleeve. Orville switched off his translator. Her musical, ancient language reminded him of a canary. The girl was insistently asking for something, but Alexandr appeared irritated and kept shaking his head. Finally he pointed to the main house and barked at the girl. She trudged away sadly.

"What happened?"

"Her favorite part of the story is when the caterpillars save their friends from drowning in a puddle near the trunk of the tree. She wanted to hear it all over again. I got the idea from the battle of Nan Madol. She has no idea how many of us died there."

Alexandr and his comrades had fought at Nan Madol, that beautiful city of stone built over a lagoon in the South Pacific, not so long ago. For the first time, the enemy had evolved a means of crossing large bodies of water: integral flotation devices. The Messengers had suffered heavy casualties, but their complete victory had prevented the enemy from further developing a transoceanic strike capability.

Orville shook his head. He had been there too, and it was something he wished he could forget. "That's no way for a storyteller to act, Alex. It isn't the listener's fault where you got the idea."

Alexandr just stared at the reflecting pool. Orville sensed that his friend was afraid he was about to lose faith in his mission. Shumina was the only person who could read his story and truly understand what he was trying to say. But it was impossible to know where Shumina's timestream might be found, if it even still existed. And his memories of her were fading. Alexandr might be close to his breaking point.

"Here's what I think you should do. Tell your story to anyone who will listen. Like the girl wanted you to, just now. What's her name?"

"I don't know," Alexandr said listlessly.

"Well then, that's the first thing you should ask."

"But if I'm just a storyteller..." His voice trailed off.

Finally he smiled resignedly, as if he had nothing left to struggle for. "Listen, Orville?"

"Yes, Alex."

"I think we've fought long enough. Is it wrong to think that?"

"It's not wrong to think that our burden is beyond bearing." For Orville that was the truth. But he had never considered giving up.

Alexandr nodded. "Maybe it's time for us to stop writing this story without end and just see if we can make as many people happy as we can."

Orville didn't answer. He watched the tiles around the reflecting pool quickly drying in the sun.

•◆•

Alexandr was court-martialed six months later. Instead of going into cryostasis, he became a wandering minstrel, reciting his epic for anyone who would listen. Cutty found him and brought him back. The charge was simple desertion. Charging him with a crime against humanity would have been more to her liking, but she wanted to be sure of a conviction.

Most Messengers voted to convict. Alexandr was returned to cryostasis, awaiting the day when a qualified legal AI could determine a punishment to fit his crime. Unless the Messengers achieved final victory, that day would never come.

Orville voted anonymously to convict. Unlike the other Messengers, he was not interested in upholding military discipline. Sending Alexandr into suspension was the only thing he could do to help his friend escape his demons.

Alexandr was probably the most single-minded Messenger of them all. He loved Shumina as a person, not as a symbol, and for that very reason he was unable to extend his love to a wider circle of creatures. Still, he was not all that different from the other Messengers. Orville was the real heretic, and he knew it. He felt a kind of envy for Alexandr, the envy someone saddled with a curse feels for another who has been set free. Orville could never forget Sayaka. He did not simply love her. He loved what she represented.

After the trial, O left Egypt and traveled the length of Asia on foot, a solitary journey of nearly a year. He navigated a storm-tossed sea in a makeshift boat, came ashore on the main island of a mountainous, nearly deserted archipelago, walked to his destination on the side of a mountain, and went into cryostasis.

One thousand two hundred and thirty years later, a roaming ET stumbled onto Mount Shiki. Orville was waiting.

Chapter 9

Orville's sword was a dazzling arc of hot blue light, slicing through anything in its path. Branches, whole trees, and the severed limbs of Reapers flew in all directions, amidst clouds of powdered snow. The air was filled with steel, rust-red iron, and solid silver body parts. From the ridge above, Miyo could hear the pulsing hum of the sword and the soft hiss of melting metal.

From the bottom of the cliff Reapers three ranks deep fired massed volleys from handheld cannons at the Messenger above. In answer to each barrage of fire, he released scores of tiny explosive projectiles from the reservoir on his hip. The bomblets met the shells of the enemy in midair and both disappeared in blossoms of fire and thick grey smoke. As the smoke drifted away, O emerged, swinging his sword, butchering the foe.

A pack of Long Leapers burst from the trees to his right and pressed the attack. This faster variant of the Jumper was nearly impossible for the soldiers to catch. The Leapers would close in on their victims from multiple directions and cut them to pieces with whiplike razors.

The blades of the Leapers and the tip of Orville's sword

were a dizzying, interlaced web of silver arcs. Heads and limbs of the mononoké flew through the air, trailing threads of blood. But the Leapers had no blood, being creatures of steel and will. The blood was the Messenger's.

Miyo looked down from the ridge above. Quietly she spoke into the *magatama*. "Are you ready?"

"Anytime," Orville replied. Miyo stood motionless on the ridge, outlined against the sky. The soldiers urged him on with continuous cheering. Silently, she cried out to him as well.

One of Takahaya's captains ran up, breathless. "We are ready, my lady." Miyo raised her staff. "Now!"

Soldiers cut ropes holding back a line of boulders positioned on the edge of the slope above. The huge stones rolled toward the valley floor with a sound of gathering thunder. At the last instant Orville leaped clear. A solid mass of boulders, snow, and uprooted trees surged past, crushing scores of the enemy.

Miyo and the soldiers ran down the slope toward Orville, who came bounding up to join them. Meeting halfway up the hill, Miyo reached out to touch the long wounds the Leapers had opened on O's arms and legs. Tears welled in her eyes. The soldiers running ahead shouted to their comrades farther up the valley.

"Cutty, where is the enemy's main force?" Orville whispered urgently. "Cutty!"

"Main force is approximately eight kilometers away. I'm sorry, that was their position seventy minutes ago. Victoria Base is under attack. I'll have to update you later."

"It will take them at least half a day to catch up." He turned to Miyo, trotting alongside, and patted her shoulder. "Don't cry. I'll be healed by tomorrow."

The Yamatai forces had tasted defeat yet again, this time at the Tsuge border crossing. The armies were in full retreat.

Swords and pikes were of little use against these new mono-noké. To hold the enemy off till spring, most of the army had gone ahead to fortify the valley. It was left to Orville and a few score men to secure their rear. For this tiny rearguard to stand and engage the mononoké was either madness or the highest form of valor. Even on the move, they were in almost continuous contact with the enemy.

A few *ri* before the mouth of the valley and the plain of Makimuku beyond, the new fortress came into view. It occupied the entire width of the valley. The position was a strong one.

"Beautiful," said Orville as they ran down toward the gate. "If the enemy were human, we could hold them off for two or three years."

"And what about the mononoké and their weapons? Three days?" asked Miyo.

Orville looked at the lowering black clouds ahead. "More than that, certainly. Look at the sky, it's sure to rain. The trees from which the ET harvest the sealant resin they use on their hides do not grow in these islands. The enemy will brave water a few inches deep, if they must, but they will not face us in the rain. We'll be able to rest at least till the weather clears." As if in answer, thunder rumbled in the distance.

Miyo noticed the soldiers carefully watching Orville's every movement. They revered him as nothing less than the god of war and followed him without question. Even the defeat in Musashino did not dim their esteem, for the Messenger himself was always victorious in single combat. Never did he allow the soldiers to see him discouraged. When Miyo thought of her own role in the fighting, she was ashamed. All she had to do was serve as a symbol. The real courage was that of Orville and the men.

They trotted through the huge main gate. Orville quickly

climbed one of the lookout towers. Kan scampered down past him and ran to join Miyo. Over his protests, she had sent him ahead to help with the fortifications. The rearguard was far too dangerous.

"How do things stand, Kan?"

"Very well, my lady. The captains are confident and all the soldiers are working hard. Not a single deserter."

"Thanks to you and the rest of our stalwarts. You should be fine without me, then."

"My lady, you mustn't say things like that," he said with a worried look.

"Why? Do you begrudge me even a nap?"

"A nap?" Kan's openmouthed astonishment drew good-natured laughter from the soldiers nearby. Without another word, Miyo walked calmly to her tent and dismissed her maidservants. Alone at last, she suddenly felt the full strain of the last several days and collapsed onto her bed. All she had here was a simple straw pallet. At her insistence, wood that might have been used to construct proper quarters for the queen went to the fortifications instead. The straw was hardly comfortable, but the moment she lay down, she felt as if her head were being pulled toward the center of the earth. The fatigue was overwhelming. While all she did was walk about and supervise the fighting from a distance, she'd still gone without rest for three days.

But before she could sleep, her handmaidens called to her in a state of excitement. "My lady, Lord Ikima is here."

"What? I will see him now." Once more Miyo forced a semblance of strength into her exhausted body. When she emerged from the tent, she was astonished to find not only Takahikoné but Mimaso and all the ministers, the entire machinery of the Yamatai state, kneeling respectfully on the snow-covered ground. Miyo looked around for Kan, but he was nowhere to be seen, so she addressed them directly.

"What is it, Ikima? Why have you brought our whole government to my doorstep at the height of this war?"

"My lady," said Takahikoné, head lowered and eyes on the ground. "The palace is virtually undefended. We would be hard-pressed to repulse a few brigands, much less a horde of mononoké. We beg you, move the armies to Makimuku."

"And strip this fortress? I can't spare a single man. The enemy will be at the gate in hours, days at most. Have you seen them? They've grown many times stronger and are coming here in force. They are terrible!"

As Miyo spoke, a knot of soldiers left the bivouac area and began walking toward her. Takahaya was with them. He must have heard that Lord Ikima was here and was coming to pay his respects.

Takahikoné did not raise his eyes. "You reason rightly, my lady, as ever. Yet it is hard to call Yamatai's capital by the name, when its sacred precincts are defended by lame old men and mere children. Give us fifty soldiers, even thirty. This I beg you."

"No," snapped Miyo, feeling exhaustion returning. "If you need men, let the ministers set aside the brush and take up the sword. Otherwise what use are you to me?"

For all her harsh words, Miyo understood Takahikoné's position. He probably needed closer to five thousand men. Winter was no time for resting by the hearth. Freed from tending their crops, the people would be laying in lumber for building, repairing farming tools, weaving cloth, making repairs to the palace and the forts at the border posts, and clearing irrigation canals before the spring rains. Not only were these tasks undone, but the previous year's harvest had been a disaster for lack of needed hands. The grain storehouses were nearly empty. Yamatai was subsisting on tribute from other chiefdoms, like a once-proud sovereign reduced to penury. For Lord Ikima and the ministers, the situation must have been intolerable.

But if destroying the enemy meant laying waste to the country, Miyo was more than prepared. If the mononoké triumphed here, there would be no palace to protect.

"If that is all you have to say, then be gone. This is no place for scholars and scribes." Overcome by weariness, Miyo turned on her heel and began walking back to the tent. But she had misjudged the depth of Takahikoné's anger. Not once had he raised his head, so she had not seen the fury boiling in his eyes. For half a year this man had been as good as stripped of power and position.

"Take her!" he bellowed. Miyo did not have time to turn before she was bound and hoisted aloft by the ministers. Her handmaidens, struck dumb with astonishment, stood rooted to the spot.

Out of the corner of her eye, Miyo spied Takahaya. She cried out to him in fear and desperation. He notched an arrow in his bow and drew it back, then stopped. Takahikoné had Miyo in his grip, and the ministers stood behind her outstretched form, using her as a shield. He lowered his bow and shouted, "Lord Ikima! What have you done?" The delegation's answer was to run, with Miyo flailing amidst them, to the gate. They were outside the fort and a few hundred paces down the path when the skies opened and a fierce downpour began. The fort behind them was quickly obscured in the rain and mist.

●◆●

They did not hold Miyo in the palace. She was taken to a small, windowless hut guarded by two soldiers loyal to Takahikoné. Her eyes were bound until she was inside, and Miyo did not know where she was. But she was neither harmed nor humiliated. Even Takahikoné hesitated to lay a hand on Himiko, Queen of Wa and Friend of Wei. Her bronze mirror and *magatama* beads were taken. No doubt Lord Ikima's future plans included a pliant replacement for the shaman queen, so he could go on ruling as before. But what would he have to rule, if the country were lost?

Miyo's guards never spoke. She threatened and pleaded for them to release her, but it was useless. After listening awhile by the door, she gave up and lay down on her bed of hard raised planks. Bitterly she admitted to herself that it was more comfortable than the pins and needles of straw in her tent at the fort.

As she passed in and out of sleep, a train of worries rumbled through her mind. Would Orville come? No, he would never leave the soldiers. They were frightened enough as it was, even with his leadership. But Kan would be looking for her. He would mount his horse and brave any weather, scouring the country for word of her.

Kan had matured tremendously under the pressure of events, but this made her fear all the more for his safety. What if he slipped into the palace in search of vengeance and was struck down himself? And would Takahaya stay with the fort? Would the soldiers stand against the enemy without his leadership? Or Miyo's leadership?

Would the fort hold?

Through months of fighting and defeat, Miyo had never allowed herself to imagine what might happen if Yamatai itself were to fall. Now, worn out and caught in a trap, the fear washed over her. If Yamatai fell, they would have no choice but to withdraw to the west. There would be nothing left to fight for, not for her men without a land, not for herself without a country. Yamatai was all she had ever known. What if those hideous monsters laid waste to everything, the way they had burned Iga and Mount Miminashi? But perhaps it did not matter. By then, Miyo would almost certainly be dead.

And the Messenger of the Laws? On his own he could escape to some place of safety. There he could wait for the best moment to return to the attack. But would he really abandon her? The thought crushed her with grief. Yet, would it not be better that he fled than be killed in a vain attempt to save her? Yes, he should escape, Miyo decided, to take revenge for those who fell in Musashino, by Lake Hamana, and in a dozen other battles.

Suddenly a terrible thought occurred to her, and she sat up. What if she were left alone in the world? It was possible, if the fort fell and Orville was killed in the fighting. Would she follow him in death? It was a Yamatai tradition. The death of a chief or an important man was always followed by the suicide of the wife. Miyo had pledged herself to him, and she was prepared for anything. But would she even be allowed to die?

She curled into a ball, surrounded by fears and regrets. Sleep refused to come.

•◆•

Toward the evening of the third day she heard hoofbeats approaching. She went to the door and strained to listen. Someone was shouting at the guards. Had Orville come for her?

She heard the guards withdraw. The door opened and a man stepped toward her. Miyo narrowed her eyes against the light streaming in behind him, then gasped. It was Takahikoné. His white tunic was spattered with mud and smeared with soot. His left arm was bare, the sleeve torn away. In his right hand he still held his sword. His hair hung loose, unbraided. Streaks of blood crossed his face.

His bloodshot eyes gleamed like a madman's. He tried to speak, but started coughing, then spat on the floor. When his voice returned, it was ravaged and hoarse.

"Himiko. I've come to take you away from here. To the west. We must pass over the Chinu Sea." He held out his hand. Miyo drew back reflexively.

"Where are the soldiers? Where is the Messenger? Are we defeated?"

"Our ruin is complete, my lady. The armies are annihilated, our palace burned to the ground."

Miyo felt the blood draining from her head. This was everything she feared. Had it happened because she had imagined it? Then this disaster was her fault! No, she must be losing her mind.

"The Messenger would never be defeated," she said finally.

"He is dead. Come, there's no time to lose." Takahikoné held out his hand again. Miyo shook her head. "Don't lie to me. The Messenger is no normal man. He cannot be killed. You must be wrong. Did you hear it from one of the soldiers?"

"I saw him die."

Her knees buckled. A strong arm kept her from falling, but in her swoon the world had left her. Orville was dead. He was gone. There was no more reason to live. For three days she had tried to prepare herself for this moment. Now it was here, and the utter senselessness of life overwhelmed her. Her mind was paralyzed. She walked outside the hut, leaning on someone for support. Suddenly the hand holding her closed like a vise. With his free arm Takahikoné grabbed Miyo in a harsh embrace.

"We will be together—at last!"

A blue object fell from his tunic and clattered to the ground. She looked down. It was the *magatama*. At once, it spoke.

"Miyo! Where are you?" O's voice. She felt a spark of joy. It was him, alive!

"It's the Messenger!" she cried. She lifted her eyes from the ground and froze. Takahikoné's face was inches from hers, mottled crimson and purple, twisted with hate. He crushed the *magatama* like a snail with his wooden sandal, grasped her waist and held her tightly. A terrible fear began crawling upward from the base of her spine.

"No! I am Himiko, sh-shaman queen…"

Takahikoné's mouth opened. His yellow teeth glistened with spittle. "That is why I must have you!" He sank his teeth into the side of her neck and ground his lips against her skin. She could feel his tongue moving, licking her blood. She reached instinctively for his one vulnerable point: his earring.

"Traitor!" She tore the ring away and blood spurted from the lobe. Takahikoné gave an unearthly shriek and threw her to the ground. She began to back away, but then he was on top of her, straddling her. She clawed at his face. He struck her with merciless force, and for an instant she lost consciousness.

"Do you know how much I've suffered?" he screamed. He grasped the neck of her tunic with both hands and tore it open. The biting wind on her skin brought her to consciousness. She threw both arms out, desperately searching the ground for a stone. Her hand closed on a small spike of wood. Quickly she brought it before her with both hands, pointed at Takahikoné's chest.

"Is that a sword?" he shouted again. Still straddling her, he pressed the point of his blade against her neck. Miyo could see her face reflected in the steel. It was smeared with someone's blood.

"You're mine now! You're mine and you always will be!" Miyo turned the point of the wood against her own throat. Her voice was a thin rasp of loathing.

"I'll die before you pollute me. I belong to the Messenger!"

Takahikoné gave a howl of anguish and rage that was almost inhuman. He tore the spike from her hands and threw himself on top of her. Miyo closed her eyes and tensed every muscle in her body.

She dimly felt a tremendous blow and heard the crunch of steel cutting through bone. Terrible pain was always preceded by momentary numbness—this she had learned from her year of war. She opened her eyes in panic. Takahikoné was staring at her in wonder, face slack, lips slightly parted. Miyo knew he could not see her. Slowly, his eyes glazed over like those of a doll. Someone stood over him, a shadow falling across Miyo's face.

Kan pulled Takahikoné's ruined body off Miyo and helped her stand. His face was haggard. She touched his cheek. "You came in time, Kan."

"Miyo!" He clasped her to his chest and buried his face in her hair. She melted in his arms. For a moment it felt completely natural. She was stunned and surprised. Finally they stepped apart. He led her back into the hut and began dressing her neck.

"The soldiers went searching for you. Lord Ikima...no, Takahikoné, shut himself up in the palace. He said you were with him, but after two days you did not appear and we forced our way in. Yes, the palace burned during the fighting. The soldiers went wild when they discovered you weren't there. They beheaded Mimaso and slaughtered the ministers to the last man. Joh is safe. I brought her out myself. Takahikoné fled. The Messenger said to follow him and we would find you."

"Then he is alive after all."

After a pause, Kan nodded. He dressed Miyo's wound gently, as if he thought she might break. "Yes. But the fort was overrun. Without you there..."

"That is grim news," said Miyo. She began examining herself for other injuries. She felt Kan's gaze. Normally she was not at all uncomfortable in his presence, even like this. But things had changed in some indefinable way. She smiled to hide her awkwardness. "I don't know how I'd manage without you."

"Serving you is my life, Lady Miyo." Kan bowed formally. She was startled; only now did she notice the simple braids at his temple, the first mark of manhood. Her strange feeling of awkwardness increased.

They left the area around the hut and walked onto the plateau. Thick columns of smoke rose in the east. Miyo saw she was on the lower slopes of Mount Nijo, on the western edge of Yamatai. "The Messenger will be here soon with the last of our men," said Kan. "Let us descend and join them." He leaped onto his horse, leaned toward Miyo and held out his hand. She climbed up behind him.

A road wound through the fields below, and sure enough a column of soldiers, their families, and crowds of people fleeing the fighting were just coming into sight. The column moved slowly but the soldiers marched in good order. In spite of their travails and weariness, spirits seemed high. They would follow the Messenger to the ends of the earth. Miyo's heart went out to them.

The two rode down the slope, stopping at the edge of the road. The passing soldiers sent up a cheer that traveled down the column. She waved and the cheers rose higher, their joy washing over her. They let the column pass and found the Messenger bringing up the rear, as she had expected.

"Miyo!" he called out cheerfully, as if being reunited with her now were the most natural thing in the world. She jumped down and ran to embrace him. "Are you all right?" he whispered.

"Yes," she answered. She wanted to say more, to tell him

that she was still his wife. But with one look, he told her it was not necessary. After a moment she said, "Takahikoné is dead."

"Yes, I knew Kan would find you," said Orville. Miyo smiled and nodded, but when she turned to Kan he was almost out of sight, riding up the column. She felt a pang of remorse. Orville reached into an inside pocket, drew out a *magatama* on a chain, and placed it around her neck. "Here's another. Try not to lose this one."

The soldiers kept turning to look at her and the Messenger as they walked side by side. "Eyes front!" she called out with forced severity. Then she said quietly, "Is there somewhere we can find safety?"

"We have to keep going," he said. "First we make for Suminoé Harbor. If boats are still there, we send the women and children west by sea and rest for the night. Otherwise we keep moving."

"And then what?"

"Don't ask."

"What do you mean?" said Miyo. "Help will come, will it not? This is what your Laws teach us." Orville was silent a long time. Then he nodded almost imperceptibly. "You're right."

Before they rounded the base of the mountain, Miyo looked back along the road. In the distance she could see the ruins of the palace on the plain of Makimuku. Thousands of tiny figures swarmed around it like iron filings around a lodestone.

Suminoé Harbor was deserted. The ships had sailed when news of the danger reached them. An old man who was left behind spoke of rumors that a large force from the west was approaching. But for now the port and its surrounding villages were silent and empty.

There were too many refugees, not enough soldiers. Miyo

decided it would be best to send the women and children west on foot, in small groups to avoid the attention of the enemy, while the men built fortifications and dug a semicircular moat around the port. The armies would have to make a stand sooner or later, and Suminoé was as good a position as any—the ground was easy to work and the fields outside the moat could be flooded with seawater. During the retreat from Musashino they had learned a bitter lesson: to keep moving only made it easier for the enemy to bleed them white. And Miyo was reluctant to move farther west, away from the land of her birth. If she was going to die, it would be here.

The soldiers seemed to be feeling the same thing. Gradually their faces became set in expressions of resignation as well as resolution. The families said their farewells, and the sorrow of parting echoed across the barren winter fields.

Three days later, a semicircular stockade had been completed, its ends projecting into the surf four hundred paces apart. The moat and the fields were flooded. That night they heard the call of approaching Snipes, and soon the air above them was filled with flying mononoké. None of Cutty's Wasps could be seen.

Just as the sky lightened and the Snipes began to fill the air like dragonflies, one of the lookouts shouted.

"They come!"

The enemy poured over Mount Ikoma and made straight for the harbor, a solid wave that carpeted the ground. Miyo climbed to the top of the stockade gate. She was adorned for a divination, her body decorated with crimson rope patterns. The stockade was lined with the remnants of the Yamatai armies, the last eight thousand men.

For over an hour, they watched as the enemy streamed in and surrounded the camp in a vast unbroken arc beyond the flooded fields. Then all at once, the enemy raised and fired their handheld cannons.

"Stand fast!" shouted the Messenger. "They have at most two volleys!"

The crash of the incoming shells drowned out his last words. Scores of soldiers were cut down. The remaining men swallowed their fear and steeled themselves for the next volley. But none came, and after a few minutes cheers went up along the stockade. The enemy's source of nitrate was two thousand *ri* to the east, in Kamaishi. Orville's guess had proven correct. They had already used up most of their ammunition during the pursuit from Musashino.

The soldiers poured out of the stockade to engage the foe on the far side of the flooded fields. They toppled the Reapers with battering rams, surrounded them and cut them down, leaped atop them and crushed their multifaceted eyes. The Jumpers were held off with swinging pikes until archers could shoot them down. The club arms of the Reapers crushed skulls and bodies. Their scythes slashed men to pieces. But the Yamatai forces pressed forward with cold fury. Atop the gate, Miyo raised her staff high and called out a war chant in a ringing voice. The winter wind carried her voice across the field and drove the men to a frenzy.

But the mononoké numbered in the thousands, and slowly they pressed the Yamatai forces back into the flooded fields. Now the men fought as they splashed through knee-deep seawater. Mononoké stumbled and fell. But instead of rising again, they shuddered convulsively and were still. Takahaya immediately began shouting, "Knock them down! Cut their tendons! The salt water is poison to them!"

Now the soldiers had a tremendous tactical advantage. Even the weakest and smallest were emboldened to fight for their share of glory. Before midday, the flooded fields were heaped with the bodies of immobilized mononoké. Saved by this fatal weakness of the enemy, it looked as if victory were finally in Yamatai's grasp. But the tides of battle turned against them.

"They're crossing the moat!" screamed the soldiers on the north side of the stockade. The moat was wide and deep, and the enemy should never have been able to breach it. But scores of mononoké had thrown themselves to certain destruction in the water so that their comrades could cross over their bodies. Suddenly the soldiers found themselves fighting inside the compound, their backs to the sea.

Then, from another part of the field a wail of despair rose from hundreds of throats. "Takahaya has fallen!"

Miyo saw him die. He had just shot down four Leapers but had run out of arrows. He picked up a huge war hammer and was in single combat with a gigantic Reaper when a Leaper came from behind and lashed out with its ribbon blade. Takahaya's last glimpse of the battlefield was from high in the air. His headless body pitched forward into the mud.

His death was the turning point. Every soldier within fifty paces froze, thunderstruck. An instant later they were all dead. Their enemy did not stop fighting.

For Miyo there was no time for grief. She jumped from her perch and ran to join the fighting inside the stockade. Suddenly she heard droning wing beats overhead and looked up in terror, expecting to see Snipes, but instead she saw a formation of twelve Wasps. Orville had saved the last of them to watch over her. They flew on ahead and tenaciously attacked the closest Reapers, sinking their teeth into their necks and crushing their fragile eyes. The men in the stockade cheered, but their cheers soon faded. The fallen RET were replaced by another wave, and then another, and the Wasps were soon destroyed.

Soldiers began streaming back through the gate. The front line crumbled. Miyo stood in the center of a semicircle of soldiers with their backs to the sea, all fighting desperately as the enemy poured in from every direction. "Miyo!" she heard above the din. She looked up to see the Messenger running toward her, pursued by a pack of Leapers.

Just then Cutty's voice came from the *magatama*. "I send final greetings to all Messengers, and to all mankind. Our last line of defense has been breached. Victoria Base will soon be overrun and I will be destroyed. But the enemy has miscalculated; they are too intent on victory. Eighty percent of the ET on this continent are within fifty kilometers of my position. I will therefore use my remaining antimatter to self-destruct. The total energy released will be 37.709 gigatons of TNT equivalent. All friendly forces must immediately move away from Victoria Base with all possible speed. All nearby stations should immediately activate protection measures for seismic and electromagnetic flux damage. Naval elements in the Indian Ocean must immediately move away from coastal zones and into deep water."

"Lady Miyo!" It was Kan. He stood with sword drawn, his back to hers. The number of soldiers was rapidly dwindling. The circle shrank. They began to crowd in around her. Death shadowed every face.

Miyo called out above the noise of battle. "Don't despair! Break out and withdraw to the beach!" The soldiers fought their way through and ran wildly for the beach a few hundred paces to their rear. Orville retreated with his back to the sea, holding off the foe as best he could. The tattered army reached the sand. "Don't stop! Into the water!" Miyo shouted. She began wading into the icy surf.

Again the voice of Cutty. "Orville and Miyo. I have your situation as of four minutes ago. I am very concerned. Your front is the weakest of all. If you fail, victory in other sectors will be in jeopardy. I regret I cannot offer you any support. With greater resources I might have been able to help you."

"What nonsense!" Miyo laughed derisively. The soldiers sacrificing their lives before her eyes seemed far more noble than this distant schemer. "All you offer are words. Is that how you fight? Don't flatter yourself. This is our battle. We will live and die without leave from you. To hell with you, you bitch of a sorceress!"

For a few moments Cutty seemed to ponder. Buffeted by the savage winter swells, Miyo ran into the freezing surf, shielded by her archers' volleys. Then Cutty spoke.

"So you think you don't need me?"

"Never!" snapped Miyo.

"I see...well, your determination is quite moving. In fact, this may even be the answer I was seeking. I failed to consider the possibility that a secure timestream might not include me."

Cutty fell silent again. Miyo could not imagine what she might be thinking. When Cutty finally spoke, her voice was filled with a sense of ease. "Thank you, Miyo. That's a fitting epitaph for me. You've given my extinction an unexpected meaning. May you be victorious." The *magatama* fell silent.

Miyo was dumbfounded. Had that stiff-necked sorceress just thanked her? She felt a sense of happiness that quickly turned to rage. How dare Cutty choose death alone!

Miyo had never seen her true form. Now she was gone, and for the first time, Miyo understood how much she had meant. This was not the end Miyo would have wanted for her. If she could only talk to Cutty once more...yes, she'd give her such a tongue lashing, the witch would be struck speechless!

The roar of continuous detonations quickly woke Miyo from her reverie. A shell whistled past her head and exploded in the water behind her. A few Reapers were firing into the soldiers milling in the surf. They had some ammunition left after all. Geysers of water mixed with smoke shot into the air. Miyo crouched lower and shouted to her men: "How do you stand?" A shout went up from the soldiers. "We stand fast!" It looked as if most of them had made it into the water and were safe. Miyo felt a small measure of relief. But by now there were no more arrows left to cover their retreat.

Miyo looked toward shore and gasped. Orville alone had not entered the water. Only twenty paces from the ocean's edge, he was surrounded by seven or eight Leapers. Their long blades struck him again and again, bringing the Messenger to his knees.

"Orville!" she screamed. The soldiers rushed onto the beach and drove off the Leapers. They carried Orville into the surf and brought him to Miyo. His body half-floated in the dark, cold water. The wavelets around him were stained crimson as they lapped at his limbs. Miyo threw herself on him, sobbing. His chest and abdomen were crossed with deep gashes. How deep, she dared not guess. He turned toward her and opened his eyes.

"Miyo..." A dry whisper. His mouth was stained with blood. "I heard you talking to Cutty. I couldn't have said it better."

"You must rest. Your wounds will heal, yes?"

"They're healing now. Just listen to me and stop crying. Look out for your people. Forget your homeland. Home is something you carry with you, in your mind. As long as you survive." He gripped her hand so hard Miyo almost cried out, but his strength reassured her.

"I understand. No more talk. You're one of the wounded now."

"Sayaka..."

"What?" Miyo started. Orville seemed to be staring into some empty place. Then his eyes fell on her again. "Ah, it's you."

Suddenly his face relaxed, as if he were about to break into a smile. His hands went slack. Miyo gripped them tightly, stroking them again and again, as if trying to stroke life into his body. Her knees began to shake.

"Orville?" She called to him, touched his face. His pale pupils no longer followed her motions. She stroked his face and wept. No matter how tightly she closed her eyes, the tears would not stop. The cheeks of the Messenger were streaked with her tears and those of the men holding him.

The wind whipped the waves to foam. Some of the soldiers dropped to their knees in the surf, exhausted. The waves of sobbing moved out from Miyo and spread to the rest of the army. The men sobbed as if the world were ending.

Then something at the core of her being rebelled. She would *not* die. She inhaled deeply, stifled the heaving in her breast, and shouted across the surf. "Raise the battle flag!" She wiped her eyes fiercely with the sleeve of her tunic and glared at the men. Their faces were shadowed with grief. She took another deep breath and shouted with all her strength:

"Raise the banner! Himiko's great war banner! I am not beaten yet!"

The men looked at her in confusion, as if they had misheard her. She raised her fists and glowered at them with red-rimmed eyes. "Rise up! We go west. The enemy cannot follow us in the surf. We will go to the lands beyond. We will swim the straits to China if we must. But we will survive! Rise up and dry your tears. Forget your homeland. As long as we live, so Yamatai will also live! The races of men will never bow to the mononoké!"

Gradually the sobbing ebbed. The men slowly moved toward her. They ignored the enemy on the beach behind them eyeing the water's edge and awaiting their chance. They gathered around her. There was no war banner. The emperor's gift had been lost in the retreat from Musashino. But one of the soldiers raised a pike with a small flag nailed to it. The flag was torn and dirty. Miyo stepped beneath it and called to her army.

"Do you swear to follow me and survive, no matter what?" The men sounded their resolve. Miyo shook her head and shouted, "Even if we must swim to China?" The men cheered again with new strength in their voices. Miyo began to walk north through the surf. "Then come with me, if you want to live!" Kan proclaimed his determination and a thousand throats echoed him. Their voices seemed spirited enough to chase the west wind out to sea.

The sky flashed white. For an instant, the landscape seemed to levitate.

Miyo looked up, momentarily blind. When her vision returned she doubted her eyes. A giant object, sheathed in armor, floated in the sky. It must have been a full *ri* or more in length, end to end. A sky ship?

Before Miyo and the soldiers were able to shake off their amazement, their upturned faces were lit again. From both ends of the ship, needles of blue-white light darted over their heads, sweeping the beach, the ruins of their camp, and the paddy fields. Wherever the needles touched the earth a wall of fire erupted, as if a fissure had opened in a volcano. The line of fire slashed across the hordes of advancing enemy. The enemy were flung end over end or torn apart where they stood. Across the battlefield, a distorted, high-pitched wailing rose to pulsing shrieks, that were suddenly cut off. The enemy was burning.

A wave of scorching heat struck Miyo. She held the soaked hem of her tunic over her nose and mouth as she silently watched. The needles of light darted out again and again. Each time, a fresh wave of heat and the groaning of the earth reached the Yamatai forces standing in the water.

Finally their eyes registered only the dancing of the blue-white light, even against the sea of fire.

The raking of the needles ceased. As their vision returned, they saw a scene from hell.

A smoldering wasteland stretched before them. The fields were now smoking pans of melted salt and iron. The bodies of the enemy lay scattered in piles into the far distance, their ruined corpses belching greasy black smoke. The smell was nauseating.

"It's coming!" yelled several soldiers at once. They watched in fear as the giant ship descended silently onto the water. Soon a small, leaf-shaped boat emerged from its side and headed toward them. A single figure stood in the prow; Miyo squinted to make him out. The man's height, build, and relaxed posture were familiar. The little boat pulled up and the man stepped down into the thigh-deep water. Miyo's voice trembled. "Orville...?"

"No. My name is Omega. I am a Temporal Army Pathfinder from the twenty-first century."

At first she did not believe him. The voice, the face—he was too similar to Orville. But when she looked closer she saw he was different. The jaw was heavier, the hair somewhat lighter than Orville's. This man was clearly younger.

Omega surveyed the results of his handiwork, then approached Orville's body, which the soldiers had laid on the beach. Omega knelt and peered intently into Orville's blind eyes. A tiny thread of light briefly linked their pupils.

"Don't touch him!" Miyo ran up, shaking with anger, and Omega quickly stepped away from the body. He spoke quietly to himself, but those nearby could just hear him:

"Messenger Original. The legends were true. How did you bear this burden so long?" He looked down at the body and raised his flat left hand to his eyebrow. Something in that strange gesture bespoke a deep respect, and Miyo stepped back.

Omega turned to her. "Did he leave instructions for handling the body?"

"For his burial? No," she answered. "But I won't let you have him."

"Then I leave him with you. Bury him with honor."

Miyo hesitated. "Are you the mighty host, the one spoken of in the Laws?"

"Yes. We came to destroy your tormenters and save this timestream for all eternity."

Miyo felt a sudden fury so terrible that everything in her sight went red. "Why now? Why not months ago, or even hours? Then the Messenger would not be dead on this beach. And Takahaya, and so many others!" She stepped toward him, fists clenched. But Omega raised a hand and calmly shook his head.

"You don't understand. We could not have come an instant before we did. The moment we arrived marked the moment our timestream came into being. This battle gave birth to it. *You* gave birth to it. He raised his hand to his brow once more and said in a voice full of reverence, "You must be Queen Himiko."

"I am."

"The Battle of Suminoé, A.D. 248. Trapped by twenty thousand mononoké, teetering on the edge of defeat, the queen of Yamatai rallies her forces and escapes to the west, where she rebuilds her army. A year later she lures a vast force of mononoké into a narrow valley, where her armies unleash a dammed river— a saltwater estuary—that drowns them all. Later, the Land of Wa flourishes under her rule, and she lays the foundations for the nation of Japan. And this becomes the prior history of a new timestream." Omega gazed at her with the affection of a child reunited with its mother.

Miyo returned his gaze and considered his words. Finally she said, "You are my distant descendant."

"I am an AI, created by your descendants. No, you are right. I am your descendant. Had you not refused to accept defeat, resistance against the ET would have collapsed on one front after another. On behalf of all humanity and human history, I thank you." Omega bowed deeply. Then he turned and sprang into the boat.

"Where are you going?" said Miyo anxiously.

"West, of course. There is work to do in China. The enemy is on the brink of victory, but that will change."

"Will you return to us?"

"No, and it is better that we do not. We came to eradicate the enemy, not to interfere in any other way with your history. We must do everything to preserve the integrity of this stream, because once the enemy is destroyed, the stream will be complete. That is our mission, no more and no less."

"And besides," he said with a laugh as the boat stirred the water beneath. "I believe you despise any form of meddling. Isn't that right?"

"Omega!"

The boat moved away quickly, was swallowed by the ship. A moment later the great sky ship rose into the air, dipped once, and accelerated out of sight. One instant it was hanging in the sky, the next there was only the echo of a titanic thrumming, like some great chord. After a long moment, it faded as well. There remained only the sound of waves on the beach and the crackling of dying fires. The soldiers stood in small groups, heads bent with weariness or staring in blank astonishment at the smoking field. Instinctively, they began to gather around Miyo.

"My queen…"

"What next?"

"What has happened?"

"We've won," said Miyo, and exhaled deeply. "Our battle cry summoned the mighty host, just as the Laws foretold. The mononoké will not come again. Our descendants have come to destroy them all."

She looked around her. The faces of the men were filled with doubt. Too much fear and suffering had been spun into a spell that would not release them. She needed something to break it. Then she saw the answer, lying on the sand.

"Let us bury the Messenger. We will build him a great tomb. Gather the bodies of the fallen and bury them together. And let us cry for their sakes, until the tears will flow no more." At these words, the men seemed to understand that everything was over. They walked slowly out of the water and up the beach.

"Lady Miyo..." Kan was beside her, his eyes brimming with tears. He spoke so only Miyo could hear. "I wished the Messenger had never come. He took you away from me. But he died so deliverance would be ours."

"Enough, Kan. It is over."

"How could I ever have doubted him?" He began to cry. His heartbroken keening carried across the beach and was echoed by other voices, first on one side, then the other, till the gray shore seemed shrouded in sorrow.

Miyo grasped his hand. She felt a tenderness for this boy as he grieved for the Messenger, and she knew their journey together would continue for many years. He was the only one who understood her.

"I'm glad you're with me, Kan." Miyo wiped her misting eyes and stared ahead. She could not afford to cry. It was time for Queen Himiko to begin restoring the Land of Wa, to watch over the tomb and honor the teachings of the Messenger of the Laws.

CHAPTER 10

The flagship *Secundus Minutius Hora* settled quietly into its sea berth at Osaka Space Terminal. Fireworks exploded in the sky and tugs sprayed fountains of water. Pathfinder Omega was on the bridge, but hardly noticed the celebration. He was absorbed in the memories passed to him on that wave-beaten shore. At first he had resisted the idea of serving as the repository for another AI's memories, but the astonishing history that streamed through his comm link erased any doubts he might have had about his assignment.

For centuries, historians believed the Messengers were the stuff of ancient legends, but in the eighteenth century they began to reexamine the old tales. Gradually it dawned on them that this strange oral tradition, stretching from Egypt across Africa and unconnected with any indigenous religion, might actually be rooted in historical fact. The stories, known collectively by names like "The Four Hundred Stream Chronicles" and "Saga of the Insect Crusade," could be interpreted as a metaphor for a temporal war extending far into the past. The oldest surviving versions of the story contained more than three hundred linked chapters. But for reasons unknown, all versions of the tale seemed to end abruptly, and investigators searched without success for the final chapter. Still, the different versions were startlingly similar, even when found in widely separated and otherwise unrelated cultures.

In the twentieth century, matters were decided in favor of historical fact when traces of antimatter were discovered deep in Africa's Victoria Crater. Until then, scientists had assumed the enormous depression was caused by a devastating meteor strike. Now it was clear that some sort of titanic struggle had taken place around 400 A.D.

Once the technology of time travel was a reality, the AIs dispatched into the past were configured for scholarly investigation as well as armed confrontation. Pathfinder Omega's ship was the first to come upon the struggle as it was taking place. Immediately, he realized the importance of recovering O's memories.

Still, the sheer size of the data partition was beyond anything he had imagined. Here was every detail of O's existence, beginning with his inception in an alternate timestream, his encounters with the ET in the twenty-second century and beyond, and his desperate struggles across more than four hundred parallel universes. Omega wandered this compendium of memory with stunned admiration. It was like a vast, silent labyrinth abandoned without regret by its builder. The riches of this data trove were beyond price, both for their scientific value and as the record of a hero's exploits.

But for Omega, such notions of value paled into insignificance compared to his direct experience of the data itself. He wandered through O's memories as if they were his own. To know such an entity—no, to inherit such a man—was a truly unexpected gift. And as the war on the ET spread from this secure universe to alternate timestreams, the lessons of Messenger O's memories were destined to play a decisive role.

Yet as he merged his mind with the data, Omega was baffled. The emotional traces he had expected to find were strangely absent. There seemed to be no pride in victory, no shame in defeat. Instead, there was a persistent thread, some residue of a thought that had carried O through untold years of striving. Whatever it was, it seemed to have been the raw material of his personality; the stuff of life that had formed the core of his being.

What is this? Omega had encountered nothing like it. It was a tiny, indefinable void, a mold once filled with something but now the essence of emptiness. The immanence of whatever had dwelt there long ago was palpable but always out of reach, like a phantom beyond the edge of his vision. It was something lost, never to be recovered, yet relentlessly pursued nevertheless.

Like a frozen caress, the void whispered its loneliness. Omega felt growing astonishment. As the core of O's self spread through his mind, he felt unaccountably happy, as if loneliness were the single emotion he associated with beauty or joy. It *was* beauty and joy. He felt a remarkable sense of peace. Was this what had driven Messenger Original for over a hundred millennia? That was something the data could not tell him.

"Are you crying?" asked the flag officer in surprise. Omega returned to the present with a jolt and touched his face. It was streaked with tears. "No. It's nothing."

"The gangway's out," said the officer brightly. "Sounds like quite a celebration." Omega rose and made his way to the portside hatch. As he stepped, blinking into the sun, onto the head of the long gangway, he understood the twinkle in the officer's eye. This was no mere celebration. It looked as if half of Japan's capital was crowded onto the space terminal's two-hundred acre apron, waving and cheering.

For the enemy, it was the beginning of the end of their reign of terror over the branching streams of human history. The species would soon reach out across time to wreak an icy vengeance, and that was reason enough for celebration. But this was almost too much.

Pathfinder Alpha stepped out onto the gangway behind him. "I might have known. The Temporals have to prove their money was well spent. It must have cost a fortune to shut down the port for this."

Omega smiled. "Oh, don't be such a cynic. This is exactly the way things were destined to be."

Alpha flashed a smile of his own, strong white teeth over which black skin stretched. "What happened to you? You're the original cynic."

"Yes. Something has changed," said Omega. He descended to the apron. The gangway ended in a large semicircle ringed by luminaries from the Ministry for Temporal Administration and the Global Confederation of Nations. Closer to the gangway was a line of young women, each holding a large bouquet of flowers. Just as Omega felt the old frown forming at the sight of all this choreography, one of the women stepped forward. When he saw her, all cynicism vanished again.

"Welcome home, Pathfinder." She held her bouquet out with slender arms. Her accent was slightly different from the lilt of standard Osakan. Her hair was jet black, her skin sun-browned. A curious, snake-like tattoo circled her upper arm in a crimson ring. Hanging from a silver chain around her neck was a single curved *magatama* bead. Omega stared; it looked like the real thing. For an instant he felt oddly disoriented. He couldn't decide whether he was looking at something ancient and barbaric or starkly contemporary. Then he realized the girl was from a region east of Osaka, where a cone-shaped mountain rose abruptly from the plain and the people carefully preserved some of the ancient forms of dress and speech.

"Listen," he said with a strange urgency. "Are you from Makimuku?"

"What?" The girl looked stunned. "How did you know? I was born there."

"And your name?"

The girl's eyes widened, and for an instant something flickered deep inside them. She stared at Omega. "Do I know you?" she said finally, a bit awkwardly.

"I doubt it."

"I'm Sayo."

"Sayo. That's a pretty name," he said. Then something inside him cried out from a place far beyond memory, like a hand stretched out longingly to touch the moon.

Just as awkwardly, he asked her, "Can I call you later?"

"Really?" Her eyes widened again. "You mean it?" She blushed. Omega nodded and took the bouquet.

About the Author

Born in 1975 in Gifu Prefecture, Issui Ogawa is rapidly becoming known as one of Japan's premier SF writers. His 1996 debut, *First a Letter from Popular Palace*, won the Shueisha JUMP Novel Grand Prix. *The Sixth Continent* (2003), a two-volume novel about settlement on the moon, garnered the 35th Seiun Prize. A collection of his short stories won the 2005 Best SF Poll, and "The Drifting Man," included in that collection, was awarded the 37th Seiun Prize for domestic short stories. Other works include *Land of Resurrection*, *Free Lunch Era*, *Fortress in a Strange Land*, and *Guiding Star*. Ogawa is a principal member of the Space Authors Club.